梁祝

Butterfly

Lovers

Butterfly Lovers

A Tale of
the Chinese Romeo and Juliet

Fan Dai

HOMA & SEKEY BOOKS
Dumont, New Jersey

ISBN: 0-9665421-4-2
Library of Congress Card Number: 99-068429

Publishers Cataloging-in-Publication Data
Dai, Fan
Butterfly Lovers: A Tale of the Chinese Romeo and Juliet
1.   China—Fiction
2.   Love stories
I. Title
PS3553.A   1999   813'.54-dc21

Published by Homa & Sekey Books
138 Veterans Plaza
P. O. Box 103
Dumont, NJ 07628

Tel: (201)384-6692
Fax: (201)384-6055
Email: info@homabooks.com
Website: www.homabooks.com

Editor: Shawn X. Ye
Cover Design: Judy Wang

First American Edition
Printed in the United States of America
1 3 5 7 9 10 8 6 4 2

For my mother, without whose love and help,
I would never be who I am

ACKNOWLEDGEMENTS

I would like to thank Homa & Sekey Books for giving me the opportunity to write this English version of one of China's oldest and most beloved folktales.

My heartfelt thanks go to Gail Gamboa Plawsky for being my personal editor. She devoted as much enthusiasm and effort in refining my prose, as I did in the writing of it.

I am indebted to Professor Judy Manton for editing and proofreading my manuscript before publication.

I especially want to express my gratitude to Stephen Smith, whose interest in the story motivated me, and whose kind offer to be its first reader before publication was a great source of criticism and encouragement for me.

My thanks also go to my husband Jigang Bao, who has always insisted that I have a talent for writing. His encouragement never fails to keep me going when I am disappointed with myself.

I would also like to thank Shitao Zhang, Xiaolei Wang, Lingyan Huang for their research assistance.

AUTHOR'S NOTE

The story of Shanbo Liang and Yingtai Zhu has been passed down as a Chinese folktale from one generation to another for the past 1,500 years or so. Most researchers agree that the story took place during the Jin Dynasty (906-960), but the story was not put into writing until the Song Dynasty (960-1279).

There have been many versions of the story in the Chinese language. They were all based on the real life story of Shanbo Liang and Yingtai Zhu who lived in Zhejiang, a mid-eastern province in China. The basic story line was the same as told in this novel.

By today's standards, and as depicted by the tragic ending of this tale, the role of woman in ancient China was a very undesirable one. For a long time, the only thing that a woman was expected or allowed to do was to stay at home and take care of the house and family. Marriages were always arranged by parents through the services of a professional matchmaker.

Such a background foreshadowed the disastrous ending of the story of Shanbo Liang and Yingtai Zhu, who fell in love with each other under the most incredible circumstances. Storytellers gave the lovers so much sympathy that they eventually romanticized their ill fortune into the butterfly fantasy.

Almost everyone in contemporary China has heard of Shanbo Liang and Yingtai Zhu, though existing written tales are few. The present novel is a combination of three available versions and the writer's own interpretation of the original story. One thing that makes this English version different from the Chinese versions is that Shanbo Liang is described as a man who was inspired by Yingtai Zhu's love and consequently fought for his own happiness. The Chinese versions place a lot more importance on Yingtai Zhu, who did extraordinary things for her time. Another characteristic of this English version is that there is a focus on the inner feelings of the characters, which is not found in its Chinese counterparts. Most likely, the lack of psychological description in the Chinese versions was due to the reservation the Chinese hold regarding emotions. Traditionally, the Chinese were not used to exhibiting affections openly, though they undoubtedly experienced very strong feelings deep inside.

This helps to explain to Western readers the emotional reservation the characters in the novel held for each other even though they were father and daughter, mother and daughter, or even lovers. In addition, young people of the time were not supposed to fall in love themselves. In fact, it would be a disgrace for a single man and a single woman to keep company without a chaperone present. Consequently, any physical contact under such circumstances would be condemned as most inappropriate.

It was also a time when women were not supposed to receive an education. Actually, there was a saying that explicitly indicated that "A virtuous woman should be one without any talent." A refined single woman from a rich family was usually confined to the house before her marriage, which meant that she would not have any chance to meet a man, let alone have a close relationship with one before the wedding took place.

Such is the background for the story of Shanbo Liang and Yingtai Zhu. Time has changed, but the story still touches the heart.

Fan Dai
New York
November 20, 1999

The story in this book took place in the
Jin Dynasty (906-960) in China

CHAPTER 1

IT WAS A bright day in early spring. Sunshine was dancing on every leaf of the willow trees and their drooping branches were bowing to the breeze. The sun had a special effect on the new roses that grew interspersed among hundreds of other wildflowers in the meadow. Their rosy fragrance seemed to be drifting in the air. The birds got so excited that their cheerful chirping gave music to the day.

This meadow overlooked the Zhu Village in Zhejiang Province. Within the village was the walled house of Mr. Gongyuan Zhu. As the most conspicuous residence in the village, the compound stood solid and proud. Inside its walls resided the most prominent family of the community. Its owner, Gongyuan Zhu, was once the chief administrator of a nearby village. After his retirement, the now wealthy Gongyuan Zhu moved his family back to the village of his birth.

Nothing could be seen of the house from outside the walls; it was designed that way. Gongyuan Zhu had had nine children. The first eight were boys, some of whom died young while others were married and had already left home. Thus, Yingtai, the youngest and only daughter, was much loved and adored, and was the sole focus, and joy of the aging Zhus.

It was mid-morning at the Zhu residence. Two young women were exiting from one of the rooms. The first girl bore an intelligent yet somewhat melancholy look upon her face, but this did not in any way make her less beautiful. Her eyes were bright, and when they blinked, they made any stranger want to talk to her. Unfortunately, they never served that purpose. Yingtai Zhu had not seen a stranger since she was twelve. She was not allowed to go out of the family compound until her parents deemed her old enough to do so. Home was where girls should be at the time.

The high-soled shoes gave Yingtai a slow and graceful walk. She wore a full-length pink dress with an embroidered belt around the waist and two wide sleeves with white fabric extensions that reached her wrists. Completing her charming look was her elaborate hairstyle. The front portion of her hair was swept back off of her face and secured with jewels, leaving the back portion of her lustrous black hair to cascade down her back beyond her waistline.

Yingtai Zhu was stepping into the garden with Yinxin, the servant girl who had been with her since Yingtai was ten. Yingtai had always treated Yinxin, one year her junior, as a younger sister, and they did everything together. As a matter of fact, they did not have anyone else if not for each other.

Yinxin was a nice looking girl clad in a light purple short-sleeved dress over a long-sleeved white shirt. A purple belt with a simple pattern of flowers encircled her waist. A couple of hair-pins kept her hair neatly off of her face, allowing the rest of her long hair to fall free and sway with each movement.

It was one of the same days: Yingtai had gotten tired of needlework and reading and suggested going to the garden, the only place where they could wander.

The Zhu family had a huge garden. More than a dozen kinds of flowers were in blossom, competing for attention.

The flowers were punctuated by a pool, an artificial hill, and a swing that had flowers running all over its stand.

Butterflies were in pairs, chasing each other amid the flowers. Among floating lily leaves, a few ducklings were swimming under the shade of the stone bridge that crossed over the pool, making loving noises to each other. Surrounding all of this and running around the inner side of the walls were willow trees with fresh leaves that were waking up to the newly arrived spring.

The lively garden lightened Yingtai's mood. She ran toward the swing and jumped onto it. Yinxin followed her, and pushed the swing to get Yingtai started.

On both sides of the swing stand crept colorful flowers that came and went out of Yingtai's sight as she swung forward and backward. She was going higher and higher, her sleeves and dress billowing in the wind. Intoxicated, she felt as if she were flying. Higher and higher she went until Yinxin got worried.

"Miss, it is getting dangerous. You might swing yourself over the stand."

"I don't care!" Yingtai's words floated down.

"But Master and Mistress do. Please, I will get into trouble!" Yinxin pleaded.

"All right, all right. I will slow down." As she said this, Yingtai gave the swing two more pushes. She closed her eyes, letting the wind whistle past her whole body.

Yinxin helped her off the swing. "Miss, I know what is on your mind. But please don't flirt with danger!"

Yingtai did not respond. Tiny beads of sweat glistened on her nose, and her face was red from the exertion of swinging.

As she sat on the swing again, a dreamy look came into her eyes.

Yinxin knew that Yingtai wanted to be by herself, so she walked away to the flower bed. Two butterflies were playing with each other, flying high and low. Yinxin held her hands up to touch them, but they adroitly twisted their bodies to pass by her. She began to chase them. Startled, the butterflies flew in two directions, like two kites whose threads were broken.

"Stop that!" Yingtai protested. "Can't you see that they were having a good time? Let them be free."

Yinxin stopped short. She looked at Yingtai. "Miss ..."

Yingtai gestured to stop her—there were men's voices on the other side of the wall!

"Who could they be? Let me have a look." As she said this, Yinxin went up the artificial hill. It was a little lower than the wall. She tiptoed, stretching herself to full length to look outward.

"Miss, come here! Four men and their servants are standing right outside the wall!"

Yingtai looked up, and said, "So what?" But curiosity was written all over her face. She was sixteen years old. Since the age of twelve, she had not been allowed to go out of the house by herself, let alone have any contact with men. She hesitated a little, then walked up the hill, and looked over the wall.

"They must be businessmen! They must be on their way to the city," Yinxin decided.

"You silly girl. Look at the way they are dressed. They are students." Yingtai corrected her.

"How can you be so sure? Perhaps I should go and ask them."

"No, don't dare! It would not be appropriate! Girls are not supposed to be out alone, especially not to see men. Talking to men would be even worse! My father would be furious if he knew this," Yingtai said.

"But he is not home! I will be right back." Yinxin flew down the hill, and went out of the back door.

Yinxin blushed as one of the men said, "Hey, look at the pretty girl!"

"Who are you, and where are you going?" she asked abruptly.

"We are students. We are on our way to Hangzhou to study."

"Why Hangzhou?"

"There is a Mr. Zhou there who is a very good educator. He has his own school up in the mountains. We want to be his students. Why not come along with us?"

Yinxin's face blushed deeper. The men did not seem to know what they were talking about—no girls went to school. But Yinxin knew Yingtai wanted to, and desperately.

Yinxin fled into the house with the men's laughter following her.

"Miss, you were right. They are students. They talked about a Mr. Zhou in Hangzhou. They want to be his students."

Yingtai's eyes brightened. "I have heard of Mr. Zhou. He taught two of my brothers."

"They were teasing me, asking me to go with them."

"That is easier said than done. They must know that women are not allowed to school." A frustrated look appeared in Yingtai's eyes. "I think I have read more than most men. But does that help? No matter how high I fly in the swing, I can never go beyond these walls. I am not even as free as the butterflies. They can come and go as they wish. Oh, Yinxin, I am going mad one of these days. I am so trapped, so trapped! Sometimes I don't seem to be able to breathe at all!" Yingtai stamped on the ground as if this could release some of the anger that was rising in her.

"We can only hope that we will be men in our next life," Yinxin said timidly, trying to comfort Yingtai.

"I don't think I can wait. It is such a waste of this life." All of a sudden, an idea flashed in her mind, filling her with excitement.

"Now, now, Yinxin, I have an idea! Yes, I will be going to school after all. I am going to convince my father that I should go to school too." Her face turned mischievous. "Yinxin, go to the sitting room and keep an eye on the front gate. As soon as my father comes back, let me know, and I shall speak with him."

CHAPTER 2

YINGTAI WAS NO ordinary girl. Though girls of her time were supposed to do nothing but housework, she received more education than even some of her brothers. Gongyuan Zhu had found several tutors to teach his sons at home. Yingtai also attended the classes ever since she could speak. Initially she was there just to play, but later she truly enjoyed learning. This was unusual, but Gongyuan Zhu did not see any harm as long as she had fun reading, reciting and writing. In fact, Gongyuan Zhu was pleased to see his little princess turn out to be more intelligent than her brothers.

However, the more Yingtai learned, and the older she got, the more frustrated she became. Eventually she lost the freedom of playing in the street which she had as a little girl. After all her brothers had left home and started a life of their own, her entire world was contained completely within the walls of the house. The garden, beautiful as it always was, represented all there was on the earth for her. True, she had two rooms to herself, one to study in and another to do needlework in, but that did not make the confinement any more bearable.

Yingtai had been pondering her future. It seemed that all she was doing was waiting to grow old enough to get married and have children. She knew that was what all women ended up doing, but she secretly told herself she could do better than that. Yet she did not know how. She would suddenly become sick of needlework, feeling she was sewing herself into even less freedom. Reading would also become a pain since it was not taking her out of the house. At times she simply became upset and angry at the fact that she was a woman.

She envied her brothers. She had become accustomed to seeing them go out and get business done. She had been asking herself and her parents why women could not do the same. Her parents' answer was almost ridiculous—"Because you aren't supposed to!" She was never convinced. She knew she could do many of the things her brothers had done, given the opportunity. But who would let her? There seemed to be a huge net in place to make sure that women could only move around in a very limited space. Yingtai found herself twisting in the net in vain—there was no way out.

Her only outlet was the swing. On it, she could push herself to a new height, letting herself fight the wind and be challenged. She experienced great pleasure doing that. It was the only thing she could control. Even so, she was still not actually going anywhere. There was a limit to how high she could go. Besides, with every forward swing, she would inevitably be dragged back. There was neither true freedom nor true escape.

Yingtai had been very unhappy trying to come to terms with her reality. But what could she do? She would love to go to school, but schools only admitted boys. It was not until that very day when the strange men teased Yinxin that Yingtai realized she could at least try her pursuit. Her heart pounded violently with expectations as she ruminated over the possibility.

An hour later, Yinxin came to tell that Master and Mistress Zhu were home. Succumbing to her eagerness, Yingtai went to her parents right away.

"Father, I want to go to Hangzhou to study," Yingtai said straightforwardly.

"Have you not learned enough with the tutors?" Gongyuan Zhu asked absent-mindedly.

"No, that is why I must go to Hangzhou."

"You are not serious about this, are you?" Gongyuan Zhu's eyes became larger.

"Yes, I am. I am very serious," Yingtai said, trying to put some determination in her voice.

"What? Are you crazy? You know that girls have never been accepted at school—not for as long as history itself?" Gongyuan Zhu was almost beside himself with disbelief.

"I will not go as a girl. I will dress myself as a man, and I will impersonate a man for as long as I am in Hangzhou," Yingtai said with great confidence.

"This is getting really ridiculous. I am not going to have this conversation with you."

"Father, please! How can you be so sure that no girls ever went to school?" Yingtai pleaded, and asked.

"Is this not obvious? Confucius had three thousand students, but did you ever hear of any women among them?"

"But is it not possible that they only thought there were no women? Perhaps there were women—but disguised in men's clothing?" Yingtai suggested almost viciously.

"You!" Gongyuan Zhu's authority was challenged, and he felt threatened. "You cannot speak to me this way! No doubt I have spoiled you too much. You are expected only to practice what every woman must—the three obediences and the four virtues." [1]

"I don't mean to upset you, Father. I am simply trying to reason with you," Yingtai said. "You have always encouraged me to learn. I am only hoping to learn more. Is this not your wish for me?"

"Stop arguing with me. I will not tolerate any more of this nonsense." Gongyuan Zhu was irritated. "Listen, from now on, all you shall, can and must do is to keep yourself home. Otherwise ..." Pacing back and forth, Gongyuan Zhu was too disturbed to go on.

Yingtai felt lost for she had never seen her father so upset. She was too frightened to speak.

Mrs. Zhu, who had been listening quietly, stood up and patted Yingtai on the shoulder. "Your father said all that for your own good, my child. Don't be so foolish. You will only be asking for trouble."

Yingtai turned to her mother. "I am not being foolish. I am trying to do what is right for me. In the past, you have always been proud of me. I don't understand why father did not even want to listen to me about this today."

"I have had enough! I will tell you this only once more: You are not going to Hangzhou. You are not even stepping out of this house. Period!"

Yingtai froze at these words. Before she knew it, tears rushed to her eyes.

"Don't cry, my poor baby." Mrs. Zhu held Yingtai to her arms.

---

[1] Obedience to father before marriage, to husband after marriage, to son after the death of husband; virtues of morality, proper speech, modest manner, and diligent work.

Yingtai let herself go and cried her heart out.

Yingtai did not know exactly how she followed her mother back to her own room. The swing and the talk with her parents must have exhausted her. She had fallen asleep before her mother left the room. When she awoke, she saw Yinxin sitting sorrowfully by her bed.

"Miss, are you feeling better?"

"I am not sure." Yingtai stood up and stretched herself. "But I have an idea."

"How to get to Hangzhou?"

"Yes. And I need your help. I am not going to eat anything until my father changes his mind. I am not going to leave this room either. When they ask about me, paint them the worst possible picture."

"And I shall sneak into the kitchen to get you food without their knowledge, correct?" Yinxin added, laughing.

Yingtai knew her parents would let her do anything she wanted to if she could find a way to make them worry about her. This confidence had made her a very persistent girl. She believed she was not being unreasonable. She had learned enough to be exposed to the outside world.

The first meal Yingtai missed did not cause much alarm because she had done that before when she was unhappy about something. Mrs. Zhu became worried when Yingtai failed to show up for the second meal. She sent for Yinxin.

"Anything wrong with Yingtai?" Mrs. Zhu asked impatiently.

"She has been refusing everything I bring to her. She looks pale too. I think she may have a fever."

"Why didn't you tell me to send for a doctor?" Mrs. Zhu's voice raised.

"She would not let me. She said the doctor could not help."

"What is that supposed to mean?"

"She said she wanted to go to school."

Mrs. Zhu turned quiet. She went with Yinxin to Yingtai's room.

"Mother, I feel awful," Yingtai said, trying to sit up in bed. Her hair was a mess, and she appeared to be very weak.

"Oh, my poor Yingtai, what are you doing to yourself?" She put her hand on Yingtai's forehead. "Are you all right?"

"I will not be until father allows me to go to Hangzhou." Yingtai knew her mother well, and hoped she could talk her father into changing his mind. "Will you speak with him about it? You know it is not fair that women are forbidden to attend school."

"All right, all right. Only if you promise me that you will eat something. If you do, I will speak with your father."

"I will not eat until father says yes," Yingtai insisted.

Knowing how stubborn her daughter could be, Mrs. Zhu lost no time to talk with her husband.

"Your daughter will die of starvation if you don't do something about it."

Gongyuan Zhu frowned. "She is not eating anything at all?"

"You know her. You know how determined she is. She always has her own way."

Gongyuan Zhu sighed. "Have we not always let her have her way? She knows us too well. She is a smart girl. She knows that eventually we will give in."

Mrs. Zhu looked at him expectantly. "So you will concede?"

"No, not really. I am trying to think of an alternative. How about this? We hire another tutor for her. It means paying more money, but we can keep her at home."

"Good idea! After all, she wants to go to Hangzhou only to study. If she can do that at home, why would she bother to leave?" Mrs. Zhu reasoned with herself, a smile coming to her face.

Yingtai did not exhibit the slightest joy when Mrs. Zhu told her about the tutor idea. "Father knows all the tutors in the area. He knows that their knowledge is limited. He knows that when someone wants to study seriously, he must go to Hangzhou."

"You are saying you still want to go to Hangzhou?"

"I am afraid so."

"So are you going to eat?" Mrs. Zhu jumped back to what she was concerned about.

"Mother, I don't want to worry you, but I simply cannot eat. You must understand just how much I want to go to Hangzhou. Please, talk to father again."

Seeing the worry and sorrow in her mother's eyes, Yingtai added a bit mischievously, "I promise I will eat again as soon as father gives his consent."

When Yingtai failed to show up for yet another meal, Mrs. Zhu could not hold it any longer.

"Oh, please, do something about it. How long do you think your daughter can go without food? "

Gongyuan Zhu started to pace back and forth in the room as he always did when he was distressed. "But she is my only daughter. I don't want her to go beyond my reach. This is a man's world! How can I let her go like this?"

"She said she would go disguised as a man!"

"That is easier said than done. Things could go wrong at any time!"

"What if… if we consult a fortune-teller?"

Gongyuan Zhu stopped his pacing, and looked at his wife. "That is not a bad idea. Get the best one in town." Educated as Gongyuan Zhu was, there was always something in him that made him listen to the fortune-teller.

Their maid, Juzi, a good friend of Yinxin, was just coming into the room, and overheard the latter part of the conversation. She went to Yinxin as soon as she could, and told her what she had heard.

"So they just need one last push from the fortune-teller," Yingtai reasoned, her face brightening up.

"I know one well, Cripple Li. He and my uncle are very good friends. He is without doubt the most popular fortune-teller in the area," Yinxin said. With this bit of news, a calculating look came upon Yinxin's face. "You will have to promise me one thing, Miss, if you want me to ask Cripple Li for this favor."

"I can promise you a million things," Yingtai said without thinking.

"Let me go with you to Hangzhou. You will need someone to take care of you."

"Done. You honestly thought I would go without you?"

Yinxin cheered at this. "I will send my cousin Shun Wang to talk to my uncle, and tell him what we want Cripple Li to do."

"Tell him what is going on here. Also tell him to say things that will make my father want to let me go to Hangzhou. I will pay him more than he ever dreamed he could ever make in one day."

Later that afternoon, when Gongyuan Zhu heard the familiar bell-ring of fortune-tellers on the street, he sent Juzi to check which one was there. Juzi came back in no time to report that it was Cripple Li.

"Let him in!"

Cripple Li limped into the Zhu's sitting room. He was not born disabled. It was said that he had made a poor living with fortune-telling. Then one day he was run over by a horse carriage and lost part of his left foot. Strangely enough, the misfortune brought him fame and consequently more customers. There was a belief that one's fortune was not supposed to be revealed, and those who revealed it would be punished in some way. Cripple Li's bad luck was considered as retribution for revealing other people's fortune, and that made people believe he was a good fortune teller who truly knew the fate of other people.

Cripple Li was wearing a long dark gray gown and very wide trousers, with a dark belt made of dark cotton cloth around his waist. He bowed humbly to Gongyuan Zhu and Mrs. Zhu.

"Good afternoon. What may I do for you today?"

"We want to find out something about one of my relatives," Gongyuan Zhu said hesitantly.

"Is this a man or a woman?"

"A woman. And she is not feeling very well at the moment," Mrs. Zhu said, making no attempt to hide her worries.

"Just give me a minute." Cripple Li put the bell down, took out a box made of bamboo, and bowed to the sky three times. He murmured something to himself with a serious look on his face. Then he gave a thorough shake to the box, opened the box, and poured six bamboo slices onto the table. The bamboo slices crossed one another.

Cripple Li cried out, "This does not look good. Not only is the woman sick, but things could get a lot worse within the next one hundred days."

"Worse?" Gongyuan Zhu asked nervously. "Is there anything we can do to stop it?"

Mrs. Zhu turned very pale. She could hardly stand without holding on to the table. "Is there anything we can do?"

Cripple Li looked at the bamboo slices for quite a while, and said, "She must go somewhere that is at least one hundred fifty miles away, and stay there for a while. Look at the six bamboo slices. They all cross one another. This means one should leave home, especially when it pertains to a woman. And this must be done very soon."

Gongyuan Zhu stiffened. He asked anxiously, "Would Hangzhou be far enough?"

Cripple Li studied the bamboo slices again. A smile came to his face. "That is perfect! Look! All the slices are pointing north. That is the direction of Hangzhou!"

"Is she too sick to leave home?" Mrs. Zhu asked.

"Has she been eating? As soon as she can eat, she will be fine," Cripple Li said assuredly.

Mrs. Zhu gave a sigh of relief. Gongyuan Zhu also relaxed.

"Thank you very much! Now please go and make yourself comfortable in the dining room. One of our staff will be along shortly, and he will bring you some silver for your service."

Cripple Li bowed, and left the room.

Gongyuan Zhu was about to say something when he heard noise from behind the screen in the sitting room. Before he could say anything, a smiling Yingtai came out, looking perfectly healthy and pleased.

"I heard Cripple Li was here. I was curious so I eavesdropped. He was correct about my sickness. I felt fine as soon as I heard him say that Hangzhou would be the right place for me to go. So, Father, when may I leave?"

"Who says you are going to Hangzhou? I just said that to send Cripple Li on his way." Gongyuan Zhu was embarrassed that Yingtai had heard the entire conversation.

"Father, you just said it. Mother heard it. I heard it. And the maid heard it. You are not going to go back on your word, are you? You don't want to see me get sick again, do you?" Yingtai got very agitated.

"How dare you ... You cannot talk to me like this!" Gongyuan Zhu's face went red with anger.

"Yingtai, you should show respect for your father. Go back to your room. Give him some time to think things over." Mrs. Zhu gave Yingtai a reassuring look, and signaled her to leave the room.

Yingtai looked at Gongyuan Zhu who sat in angry silence. She knew this was a good sign. She gave her mother a wink, and left without a sound.

After dinner that evening, Yingtai was summoned by her parents.

"Yingtai, I hope you understand that this is an absolutely crazy idea. I can make a decision in your favor only if you abide by three conditions." Gongyuan Zhu started with a solemn look on his face.

"I can do more than that." Yingtai's face glowed with delight.

"Firstly," her father continued, "you have to be extremely careful in the way you dress, in the way you speak, and in the way you behave. If people were to discover that you are a woman, it would bring disgrace to the Zhu family."

"Father, this will not happen. I had dressed like a boy many times in my childhood, and I grew up observing how my brothers spoke and behaved."

"Secondly, your mother has been in poor health in recent years. It is not a good idea for you to leave home for too long. Therefore, if she begins to ail, you must come back as soon as you are notified."

"Of course I will, Father."

"Thirdly ... thirdly, well..." Gongyuan Zhu looked a bit embarrassed. "This one will be most difficult for you."

"As long as I am allowed to go to Hangzhou, nothing will be too difficult," Yingtai assured him.

"All right then. Since you will be away for a while and you will be beyond our control, you must behave with honor, and not do anything stupid or shameful. When you return, I will have you checked out medically. If you remain a virgin, then everything will be fine."

"Otherwise?" Yingtai could not help asking.

"You know that too well. Otherwise you will have to find a way to kill yourself."

"Well, well, I thought you were going to make me do three impossible things. All you have made me promise to do is what I would normally do as a daughter and as a woman. There will be no problem. I will do exactly what you asked of me."

Mrs. Zhu felt bad for Yingtai as her husband was making his points. Seeing that Yingtai handled the situation with ease, she drew her daughter to her arms.

"That is my good girl! When do you think you will leave?"

"I will let father decide."

"Now that I have decided to let you go, it does not make any difference whether you leave in five or ten days. Tomorrow, you can change into man's clothing and get used to living like a man. You can leave when you feel comfortable behaving like a man. Take Yinxin with you. Needless to say, she too will have to dress like a manservant."

"Thank you, Father! I was about to ask whether Yinxin could go with me. She will be a great help to me."

"Shun Wang will leave a day earlier than you with your luggage so that Yinxin does not have too much to carry on the road."

"Thank you very much, Father." All of a sudden, things seemed too good to be true for Yingtai.

The next day, Yinxin went through the wardrobe to look for clothes that the Zhu brothers had left behind. A tailor was called in to take the clothes in to fit both Yingtai and Yinxin. Yingtai tried on a light yellow long gown that students and educated men wore. It hung down to her ankles with two long slits on both sides, giving her a scholarly demeanor. Yinxin fixed her hair, making two small bunches of hair on her temples, letting the rest fall down naturally. She wrapped a scarf around the upper part of Yingtai's forehead, and used two pins to fold the scarf toward the top of Yingtai's hair to make it stand upright, forming a crown-like cap.

"Wow, Miss, you make a very handsome young man!" Yinxin exclaimed.

Yingtai looked at the piece of bronze that served as a mirror, and saw her reflection in it: her female face changed magically to a good-looking male face simply with the change of clothes, yet her feminine nature added a fine touch to her face that made her more attractive than an average handsome man. The trick seemed to be mainly in the collar: men's clothes did not really have a collar; instead, the front left side, which was wider than the right side, would go diagonally over the latter. She smiled to herself. She could almost see herself among a group of men in her new apparel. She had not realized that the way one dressed could make such a big difference in one's overall appearance.

The next few days saw Yingtai and Yinxin busy learning to be men. They held their voices so that they could produce lower pitched sounds. They changed the way they walked to be more manly. Yinxin had great trouble getting used to calling Yingtai "Master." The two of them laughed and laughed at suddenly "becoming" men, thrilled at the fact that they would soon be out of their long-term confinement and set free. The change to their lives came so quickly and so dramatically that they could barely adjust their thoughts and behavior.

Yingtai found herself so excited that she did not know what else to do except learning to be a man. All she had read about studying at school and of traveling about the country consumed her, and completely occupied her thoughts. She had longed to live like that forever, but was never able to picture herself truly living out that fantasy. Her father's decision to allow her to actually go to Hangzhou was definitely the fulfillment of all her fantasies and dreams.

When he saw Yingtai in man's clothing, Gongyuan Zhu commented on her appearance, and reiterated the importance of really looking and behaving like a man. Both he and Mrs.

Zhu were pleased to see that Yingtai could indeed pass as a male student.

Mrs. Zhu had much advice to give, often punctuated by tears, especially when the reality of Yingtai's leaving home for three long years sank in.

Four days later, everything was ready for the trip. Yingtai, a blue scarf on her head and a long blue gown stretching to her ankles, appeared like a refined young student. Yinxin was wearing a long light green gown and a pair of green trousers, with a dark green belt tied around her forehead and another one around her waist. Her hair was in two pigtails that men wore—she looked like a typical manservant.

Yingtai bowed to her parents. "How do I look?"

"You look like a man all right now. But remember you have to look like this for many days to come. What is most important is you do what you have promised," said Gongyuan Zhu sternly.

Yingtai nodded. "I will not forget."

Yinxin also bowed to Gongyuan Zhu and Mrs. Zhu.

"Take good care of your Miss, er…no, Master. Make sure you call her Master from now on," Mrs. Zhu said.

Yingtai and Yinxin made their way to the front gate. The servants had a horse ready for Yingtai outside the gate. "Please stay indoors, Father and Mother. I promise everything is going to be fine." Yingtai urged for she did not want to see her mother shed any more tears.

At seeing Dark Red, the finest horse in the Zhu stables, Yingtai became excited. It had been a few years since she was allowed on a horse. Now she would be riding one for several days! She signaled to the groomsman to bring the horse over to her. Yingtai took the reins, and mounted Dark Red as expertly and quickly as if she had been riding all along.

She turned around and found her parents standing by the horse, her mother red-eyed and her father fighting to keep his composure. A wave of emotions flooded over her. Tears rushed to her eyes. She had never been away from them, let alone left home for a strange place for such a long time. For an instant, she almost lost the courage to go.

Yingtai checked herself. She knew it was either now or never. She shook her head sadly. Leaving no time for her parents to say anything, she waved them good-bye while signaling the horse to go with a gentle squeeze of her thighs.

"Please take good care of yourselves. Someday you will be proud of me," she whispered, without looking directly at her parents.

Yinxin followed the horse, carrying two bags on her shoulders. It was only when they were turning around the corner that Yingtai could trust herself enough to look back. Her parents were still standing by the gate, her mother waving and wiping her eyes ...

CHAPTER 3

YINGTAI AND YINXIN had been travelling quietly for a long while until Yingtai broke the silence.

"Is the luggage getting heavy?"

"No, it is not a very heavy load. You know Shun Wang had taken most of the luggage."

Yingtai was quiet again. Then she said, "I have not had a chance to enjoy the outdoors for a long time. Why don't we take it easy and travel at a more leisurely pace? I want to see and touch the flowers. They are at their best in early spring. What do you think?"

"That is a wonderful idea!"

Both of them laughed and cheered up. Yingtai stretched herself on the horse.

She started to feel relaxed as the tension and sadness of leaving home was fading away. Looking far into the horizon, she was thrilled by a sense of freedom that had been absent from her life for as long as she could remember.

"My, it is wonderful to be able to travel as freely as a man! It is so beautiful out here!" she exclaimed.

"Miss, do you want me to pick some flowers for you?" Yinxin went to the roadside, ready to gather up some of the flowers that were dancing in the breeze.

"Oh yes, please do!" Yingtai said without thinking. "Oh, wait a moment! What did you just call me?"

Yinxin realized her mistake. "Sorry, Master." She made a face at Yingtai.

"And I guess I must not exhibit such feminine interest in the flowers," Yingtai said dejectedly.

"But no one is around. You can even get off the horse and go crazy for a while. I will keep watch for any strangers."

"Are you sure?" Yingtai was very much tempted.

"Do you recall seeing anyone thus far? This part of the country is pretty deserted," Yinxin assured her.

No sooner had Yinxin finished these words than Yingtai dismounted the horse. She walked to the roadside and ran her hands over the flowers. "Oh, this feels so different from touching the flowers in our garden!" she cried. She stepped a little way into the meadow, where grass and flowers grew abundantly. She bent to smell them and breathed in the earthy aroma of the grass and the mixed fragrances of the varied flowers.

"Mmm, I never knew that grass and flowers could smell this good!" she cried out into the field in a voice that was louder than she had ever used. Turning back to Yinxin, she said, "I had almost forgotten that the world is so vast!" She looked up to the sky. "Even the sky is bigger!" She stretched her arms high up as if she could catch the clouds.

"You look so beautiful, no, so handsome there!" Yinxin commented.

Yingtai's face turned very red at that. She became more excited and began to spin about in all directions in order to experience her newfound freedom to the maximum.

"Mis ... Master, we had better get moving on." Seeing Yingtai getting a little too animated, Yinxin began to worry.

"So soon? I have just begun to play!" Yingtai complained.

"What if someone sees us?"

"All right! I suppose I can experience this every day from now on," Yingtai said, reluctantly walking back to the road.

Suddenly she threw herself down into the carpet of wild flowers and rolled about with wild abandon.

"Master, Master! What are you doing? You are beginning to frighten me! Be careful! You could be cut by the rose thorns!" Yinxin cried anxiously.

Yingtai emerged from the flowers, laughing and trying to catch her breath from the sudden exertion. "That was so ... much fun. I wish I ... could do this all the time!"

"But this is going too far! Besides, you might hurt yourself! Come back here, please!" Yinxin protested.

"All right, you win. I guess I just don't know how to handle so much freedom after leading such a secluded life." Yingtai collected herself and headed back toward the horse, beaming excitedly.

They stayed at an inn that first night. Everything had gone well on the road the next day until afternoon, when a thunderstorm threatened. The nearest hotel was still a half-hour away, so they decided to take shelter under a thatched pavilion by the road.

Yingtai got off the horse and stepped into the pavilion while Yinxin tied the horse to one of the big willow trees nearby. Yingtai looked around and saw several patches of land with different crops. The wind was blowing hard and the stems of the crops were bending from one side to another, a kaleidoscope of moving colors.

FAN DAI

"Gorgeous!" Yingtai exclaimed.

Yinxin stepped into the pavilion and ran her gaze near and far at Yingtai's comment.

"Look, two people are heading our way. It looks as if they are coming for shelter too."

Shanbo Liang and his servant Sijiu were hurrying toward the thatched pavilion to escape the impending storm. They too were on their way to Hangzhou. Shanbo was dressed in the same kind of long gown that Yingtai wore, with the same kind of cap made from a scarf. The only difference was that his clothes were made of lesser quality material. It was apparent that Shanbo was not from a wealthy family.

Shanbo's horse was not a strong one. In fact, it looked rather sickly and aged. His gait was such that he looked even more fatigued than Sijiu—and Sijiu was walking and carrying luggage on both sides of a carrying pole.

Shanbo was thinking of taking a brief rest when he spotted the pavilion up ahead. With the sky turning darker, he urged the horse to go faster.

"Master, there are people in the pavilion." Sijiu, knowing his master's unease with strangers, panted this warning. Sijiu found that talking was difficult while carrying such a heavy load.

"That is all right. They look like nice people. You can place the luggage to one side and rest with me."

Shanbo got off the horse and walked up to the pavilion. Yingtai nodded to him politely. Bowing to her slightly, Shanbo said, "I hope you will not mind our intrusion. We are here to take shelter for a while."

Yingtai returned the same courteous gesture and said, "No, not at all. We are not doing anything here, just taking a rest and waiting for the rain to cease."

Suddenly they all heard the frightened and hostile whinnying of horses. Shanbo walked out and asked, "Sijiu, what is the matter?"

"Oh, he has frightened our horse!" Yinxin cried unhappily.

Sijiu had tried to tie Shanbo's horse to the same willow tree that Dark Red was hitched up to. This frightened the younger horse and his protest was what they all heard. Yinxin rushed to calm Dark Red down.

"Hey, horseman, where are you from?" Sijiu asked.

Yinxin glared at him and went on about her business.

"Hello, did you hear me? Have you lost your voice?"

"Shh! You are making too much noise." Yinxin said between her teeth.

"Why didn't you answer my question?"

"Because you are rude. I don't care for the way you addressed me."

"Sijiu, this is not the proper way to begin a relationship. You should apologize to this young man." Shanbo interjected.

"Sorry, Master, I only thought that the horses could keep each other company," Sijiu said to Shanbo. Turning to Yinxin, he bowed, "I am terribly sorry. I did not mean to be rude. I was merely joking with you when I called you 'horseman' because you had the horse under control. Please accept my apology." Sijiu bowed again, smiling.

Yinxin smiled too and bowed back to him.

"My name is Sijiu. I am going to Hangzhou with my Master."

"My name is Yinxin. I am going to Hangzhou with my Mi ... Master too."

Yingtai and Shanbo heard the exchanges between them and smiled at each other.

"Let me introduce myself. My name is Shanbo Liang. I am going to Hangzhou to study under a Master Zhou, Shizhang Zhou. He has his own school there and I want to be his student."

Yingtai could not help showing her joy at hearing this. "That is exactly the reason why I am going to Hangzhou as well. I have heard that Master Zhou is a great educator and I want to be his student too!"

"That is what I have heard also. I hope he does not refuse us. I am sure he already has many students. Let us hope that he has room for two more."

Then they exchanged the names of their villages and found that their villages were not far apart. Four hours by horse was enough to get from one village to the other. Shanbo told Yingtai that he was the only child of the family and envied Yingtai for having siblings.

"But when I get to Hangzhou, I will have no relatives or friends," Yingtai said, thinking this might be some kind of consolation for him.

"Neither will I."

"But we now know each other. We can help each other."

"Miss ..." Yinxin started.

"What is wrong with you today, Yinxin? Your Miss is at home." Yingtai cut her short. Before anyone had time to think, Yingtai came up with a story.

"Life is so unfair for women. We men can go to Hangzhou to study if we choose to, but women cannot. My poor sister, the only sister I have, wanted very much to come with me to Hangzhou. She has read every book I have read. She is a very intelligent girl, but my father would not allow her to accompany me."

"That is really too bad. But you know, such unfair practice has existed for centuries. It looks highly unlikely that it will change within our lifetime. Tradition is tradition." Shanbo stated.

"I know. But there have been women scholars in the past. Take Ban Chao back in the East Han Dynasty for example. She was a great writer and she actually finished writing her brother's 'History of the Han Dynasty' after his death. She could not possibly have been self-taught; she must have studied with some teacher. And then there was Cai Wenji during the same dynasty. She was also very well versed in literature and she wrote great poetry. It is a bit hard to believe that she learned it all by herself. I am sure she too must have had a teacher." Yingtai declared.

"You have made some very good points. You should marry an educated woman and she should open up a school for women." Shanbo commented jokingly. Then he recited a poem by Cai Wenji.

"You know her poetry well," Yingtai said admiringly. "I am glad that you are sympathetic to women."

"I never gave it much thought, to be honest. You made me feel sorry for them. Good for you to think of them."

"I probably would not think this way if it were not for my sister. It pains me to think that she is going to waste all of her intelligence by staying at home for the rest of her life. All she is doing is sitting at home and waiting to be married off. It's just not fair."

As Yingtai was talking, she felt as if she really had a sister. Now that she had left home, her confined life must belong to somebody else.

Shanbo did not say a word, but looked at Yingtai thoughtfully. Yingtai was seized by a sudden attack of shyness. Her face turned red. She did not want Shanbo to notice the change so she turned to look out at the fields.

By this time the rain had stopped and Shanbo's attention shifted.

"I guess we had better get going," he said. "I am so glad that we met. What a coincidence." He hesitated a moment and then said, "But there is something else I really would like to say."

"Please go ahead. I feel we already know each other very well."

"Master Zhou must have a lot of students from different places. They must speak different dialects and have different lifestyles. Since we share the same dialect, it would be a lot easier for us to study together."

"This is exactly what I was thinking of. We could discuss and review what we will learn together."

"I am glad you agreed. By all means, let us do it then," Shanbo responded happily.

CHAPTER 4

THEY TRAVELED FOR three more days, but the trip was never boring. Yingtai and Shanbo enjoyed each other's company. The flowers and fresh air of the spring made everything more beautiful. They had a lot of fun taking turns creating poetry about whatever caught their interest along the road. One of them would give one line and the other would give another. They went on until they had a four-lined poem. This was a pastime that the learned enjoyed doing together. Yingtai used to play this way with her brothers. However, this was the first time she had ever played with someone outside her family. Before too long, she had the feeling that Shanbo was becoming like a brother to her.

Shanbo was in high spirits. This was his first long trip from home too. His parents never wanted him to be out of their sight. Besides, they could not afford to let him study somewhere else. He had been a little worried about what would lie ahead, but Yingtai's presence made everything more interesting and his worries were slowly fading away as he came to know more about him. There was something special about this young man that attracted him, though he could not pinpoint exactly what it was.

When they got to Hangzhou, they stayed in the hotel where Yingtai's other servant Shun Wang was awaiting with the bulk of her luggage. The next morning, Yingtai and Shanbo headed toward the mountain where Master Zhou's school was located.

Soon the school came into view. A white wall encircled the whole place, with hundreds of bamboo bending over from inside the wall. Wild flowers were scattered everywhere. Birds were flitting from one branch to another. Other than the birds' songs, the school campus was very quiet, so quiet that the air itself seemed to be holy. Yingtai and Shanbo exchanged an excited look and smiled to each other: it was close to their shared imagination and they could almost smell the books.

They walked to the gate. The gatekeeper came out and asked, "May I help you?"

"Yes. My name is Shanbo Liang and this is Yingtai Zhu." Shanbo stepped forward and bowed politely. "We are here to see Master Zhou. It is our fondest hope that he will take us on as students. Will you arrange for us to see him?"

"Yes. Let me go in and tell him that you are here."

He returned a few minutes later and signaled them to follow him.

Yingtai looked around as they walked along the pebbled path through a garden. There were bungalows with thatched roofs in all directions. She thought to herself that they must be classrooms because she could see quite a few young men reading or discussing within them. Her heart was filled with extreme excitement and her footsteps were almost unsteady—she could not believe that she was now in a man's world, a place she was never meant to be.

"This is so nice. How many students does Master have?" she asked. She felt she had to say something. Otherwise, they would hear her heartbeats.

"More than a hundred. They are from all over the country."

"I hope he will take us," Shanbo said.

"As far as I know, he never rejects any student, that is, if he is convinced that he will make a good student."

They soon found themselves in front of a large house. "Master Zhou's office is over there," the gatekeeper whispered to them.

Yingtai became very nervous. Would Master Zhou like her? Would he discover her secret? She could not help walking closer to Shanbo as if this would give her a better chance.

Soon they were inside the room. In the middle was a big wooden desk piled high with books. Behind the desk were rows of bookshelves also filled with books. A middle-aged man in a long dark blue gown and a dark blue scarf, the same style of clothing that Yingtai and Shanbo wore, was standing by one side of the desk.

"This is Master Zhou," said the gatekeeper. "This is Shanbo Liang and this is Yingtai Zhu." He turned to Master Zhou introducing the two newcomers. Then he turned and left the room.

Yingtai and Shanbo bowed to the Master, to which Master Zhou returned the bow. Yingtai took the first good look at Master Zhou. He was bearded, typical of scholars at the time.

"Please sit down and tell me your backgrounds and why you are here," Master Zhou said in a very straightforward way.

Yingtai gave Shanbo a look to urge him to speak first. This was, after all, her first time out alone in an all-male world. She was afraid of making mistakes.

"I have long heard of you and have always wanted to learn from you," Shanbo started, "but my parents had thought I was too young to leave home until this year. They decided that I should not wait any longer. I met Yingtai on the way. It so happened that he was also heading here. So we traveled together for the rest of the journey."

Master Zhou absent-mindedly stroked his beard, nodding as Shanbo talked. He could tell that the two young men were intelligent, yet he noticed that there was something about Yingtai that made him somewhat different from other students. So he asked, "Yingtai, tell me why you are here."

"I heard that you are a great teacher. This is a time when the country needs educated people. I want to learn more so that I may do something useful when needed." Yingtai heard herself say this, making a great effort to keep her pitch low and to fight the uncertainty in her voice. She tried to be vague about what she said.

A faint but reassuring smile came to Master Zhou's face. He then asked the routine question, "Did you bring anything you have written?"

Yingtai and Shanbo said yes. They had known this was a must for admission.

They each handed one article to Master Zhou.

Master Zhou read the articles carefully twice while Yingtai and Shanbo sat in anxious silence awaiting his comments. They exchanged looks and then smiled a bit nervously to each other. Shanbo observed Mr. Zhou's facial expression as the teacher looked out of the window. Yingtai had at least one reason to be more worried than Shanbo: her paper was never graded or commented on by any tutor except her father, who always praised her writing out of paternal pride. She tried to fight her growing apprehension by fixing her eyes upon the floor and then by rubbing her hands together. She soon realized that these actions could be seen as too feminine, so she quickly moved her eyes toward the window when she saw Shanbo direct his attention in that direction.

"Wonderful! You both write very well." Mr. Zhou concluded before the silence became unbearable for Yingtai.

"I am happy to accept both of you as my students. We have one hundred and ten students here. I conduct classes every other day, normally on odd days. Do you see that big hall behind this room? That is the lecture room where I teach. Students read and study on their own on even days. I am also available for questions on these particular days. If you have questions or problems, don't hesitate to come and see me in my office."

Yingtai and Shanbo were relieved and overjoyed. They thanked Mr. Zhou gratefully. Yingtai was almost in tears and said to the Master, "I cannot tell you how much this means to me."

A simple ritual was conducted. While Master Zhou sat at his desk, Shanbo and Yingtai bowed to him four times each, officially inaugurating the teacher-student relationship.

"Since you have already become good friends, you may want to live close to each other. I think there are still two rooms adjacent to each other that are unoccupied. They are only a few minutes from here. I will have a member of the staff make them ready for you and then take you over there. They will serve as your bedrooms as well as studies."

"Thank you very much. We have brought our servants with us. Would it be possible for them to have separate rooms near ours?" asked Shanbo.

"I think so. There should be some smaller rooms opposite yours. This will make it easy for you to call your servants."

Yingtai and Shanbo thanked Master Zhou again and left.

The next day, they checked out of the hotel and moved into the school. The rooms had been tidied up for them. The two rooms were more than adjacent to each other; they were in the same apartment. There were two yards, one in the front and the other in the back. A communal bathroom was just down the hall, with the kitchen beyond that. Chefs prepared food in the dining hall where most of the students gathered to eat. They would also prepare special orders to go for those students who wanted to eat in their quarters and were willing to pay the additional cost.

The place was well shaded: two huge camphor trees guarded the front yard, two bending willow trees arched in the backyard, with rows of bamboo around them.

The rooms were furnished with beds and desks. Yingtai walked through the first room which led to the second room. "Shanbo, this room is very nice. You should take it."

Shanbo followed her into the room. "Yes, it is very nice. But I would like you to take it if you prefer."

"I would prefer to take the other one," Yingtai said as she walked into the other room. "Oh, no!" She burst out a little nervously.

"What is the matter?" Shanbo, who could not see anything wrong, asked in puzzlement.

"There is no door in this room that opens to the backyard," Yingtai complained.

"But you can go to the backyard from the front door. I know it is not as convenient, but I guess you will not always want to go out into the backyard," Shanbo suggested.

"Well, you are probably right," Yingtai paused for a while. She knew she was overreacting: a man would not worry about something like this. She told herself that she had to be careful with what she said. "But there are two of us. I don't want to disturb you by constantly going through your room every time I want to get out. Let us talk to the housing staff and ask them to seal the door between our rooms and install an outside door in my room so I will not be such a bother to you."

Shanbo was a bit surprised, but said, "OK, if that is what you want. But I really don't mind the way it is now."

On second thought, Yingtai realized her suggestion was ridiculous. If Master Zhou put the two of them together like this, that meant he believed that they were closer to each other than other students. If she insisted on changing the door, that would create a strange space between Shanbo and herself. She decided that she must not give away her secret of womanhood while trying to keep it.

"Oh, forget it. I am just being stupid. It is really not worth the trouble. I was just worried about inconveniencing you. If you say you will not mind, why should I worry about it? This arrangement will be just fine as it is."

Shanbo did not quite understand her and said nothing.

"Let us go and see Yinxin and Sijiu's rooms now." Yingtai thought it a good idea to divert Shanbo's attention.

Yinxin and Sijiu's rooms had similar settings except that the rooms were smaller. The two were busy unpacking.

"How do you like it here?" Yingtai asked Yinxin.

"Good, only the wall needs some work. See, Sijiu can actually peep through the slits and look into my room."

"Why would I want to do that? I can see you better walking into your room." Sijiu snapped.

"You are right, Sijiu. Yinxin has had this weird fixation since he was little. He has always worried about other people peeping at him." Yingtai said half jokingly.

"Well then, I promise I will never peep," Sijiu said.

At the first chance she could, Yingtai went with Yinxin to check out the bathroom. Since there were no women in the school all the restrooms were for men. The waste facility consisted of no more than a bucket. Though it did not provide much of a shelter, each bathroom had only two buckets in it, which meant that Yingtai and Yinxin did not have to worry too much about being inconvenienced by other people when they used the restroom.

"Well, we just have to take turns watching out for each other when we use the bathroom. As for washing ourselves, we will have to do that in the room and make sure Shanbo and Sijiu don't see us," Yingtai continued, "thankfully this is too personal for Shanbo to want to share with me." Yingtai could not help saying this and she blushed.

Yinxin was still a little worried. "What about our clothes? When we wash our clothes, we have to hang them out in the backyard to dry. You know, there are certain items that only we use."

"Just hide them under the outer clothes. Mind you, this is the most tale-tell part. You will have to literally wait in the back yard for the clothes to dry, to make sure Shanbo or Sijiu never come close enough to see anything clearly," Yingtai said solemnly. "Otherwise you and I will have to go home."

It did not take long before Yingtai and Shanbo settled down. Both chose to place their desks by the window. The camphor trees gave Shanbo's room a lot of shade and breeze while the bamboo outside Yingtai's window gave her room a fresh touch, with a few bamboo leaves pushing into the window. They could sit close to nature and read during the day. In the evening they would read by candlelight.

Every other day they would go to class. Master Zhou divided his students into two groups, giving different lectures to the morning and afternoon classes. Yingtai and Shanbo were in the latter, always sitting in the front row next to each other.

Days went by.

One evening, Yingtai was lighting a candle when Shanbo came into her room.

"I was thinking ..." he said with a little hesitation in his voice.

Yingtai turned to him in quiet encouragement waiting for him to continue.

"It is a waste of candles for us to read in our own rooms. Why don't we use the same desk? We can save half as many candles. What do you think?"

Yingtai could feel her heart beating faster at the idea. She knew she should say no as a woman, but she was supposed to be a man and she liked the idea of reading with Shanbo.

"Well, maybe I care more about saving on candles than you do. After all you are from a rich family. What is a few savings to you?" Seeing that Yingtai did not answer right away, Shanbo became upset. "Just forget what I said."

"Oh, no, I think that is a great idea. I wonder why the idea never occurred to me. You are so clever Shanbo. Yes, let us start today!"

"Are you sure?" Shanbo smiled.

"Absolutely." Yingtai noticed that Shanbo was very aware of the difference between their family backgrounds and was determined not to hurt his feelings.

Having said that, Yingtai moved the lit candle to Shanbo's desk. They sat opposite each other and began reading. Yingtai was amazed to find that she could not concentrate at all. The fact that Shanbo was so near her had a strong impact on her. She was never so close to Shanbo and for so long. She kept stealing looks at him. For the first time, she could see the details of his features. She decided he was very handsome. His eyes were not very big and his lips were thick. Yingtai smiled to herself: people tended to think that men with thick lips were reliable. Shanbo was definitely a reliable person. Shanbo leafed a page. He was reading very attentively. Yingtai then realized that she had not been reading at all. Her face went very red as if Shanbo had discovered her secret. She hoped that Shanbo would look at her, but was also worried that he might find her behavior weird. Yingtai smiled to herself. How would he react if he knew she was a woman? She played with the thought for a while and made an effort to force her eyes off Shanbo.

CHAPTER 5

AS TIME WENT by, Yingtai and Shanbo began to be known as inseparable friends: they lived together, read together, took walks together after dinner ...

"You two are like brothers," their classmates commented.

Yingtai and Shanbo smiled and looked at each other.

It was raining before dinner one evening. Taking a walk after dinner would be out of the question. Yingtai was looking out of her window at the willows when Shanbo came to her.

"I like the fresh look of the willows in the rain. It reminds me of the afternoon we first met before the rainstorm. The willows around the thatched pavilion were exactly like this," Shanbo said.

"Indeed," said Yingtai. "I love the greenness of the willows. It fills me with so much life."

"Yingtai, people have been saying that we're like brothers. I do think that we're in many ways connected. I have been thinking of something, but I cannot bring myself to talk about it."

"As you said, we are like brothers. There is nothing we cannot talk about. Please say it." Yingtai's heart started to beat faster. Could it be that Shanbo knew her true identity?

"I was hoping...hoping that we could become sworn brothers. That would create an even stronger bond between us."

Yingtai's eyebrows raised. "Yes, we should. I would love to be your sworn brother."

"However, I do want to talk about one thing before we do this. We are from very different backgrounds. Your family is rich and mine has always been poor. Will you be uncomfortable with the idea of having an impoverished brother?"

"Of course not. Is that not apparent after all these months?"

"Yes, It is. That is why I suggested the brotherhood in the first place. But people from families like ours are not supposed to have such a bond, I mean, this is the tradition."

"But we are different from others. Our relationship can go beyond the traditional practice."

"Yes, this is how I feel too. Yingtai, in fact, that is something that distinguishes you from any other person I have ever met. I resent those from rich families who think they are better human beings just because they have more money. But you are not that type. You judge people by who they are, not where they are from. I appreciate your friendship more than anything else and I respect you a lot."

Yingtai was very touched and flattered. "Shanbo, I respect you too. You never have to feel inferior because of your family background. You are who you are. You should be proud of yourself. I am glad we have become such good friends. Although I already have several brothers, I can certainly welcome one more!"

"Thank you, Yingtai." Shanbo was overwhelmed by Yingtai's words. He put his hand on Yingtai's shoulder to show his affection.

A strange feeling stirred in Yingtai. She could not move and dared not repeat the gesture to Shanbo. She looked at Shanbo in confusion and then quickly tried to get the conversation going once again.

"I am seventeen years old. And you are eighteen?"

"Yes, that makes me the older brother," Shanbo said.

"So now you have yourself a younger brother," Yingtai said.

"Where should we hold the ritual?" Shanbo looked around.

"This room is a good place. You see, we are looking at the two willows, with so much bamboo surrounding them. This symbolizes that our bonding has as much life as they do."

Yinxin and Sijiu were called in to move the desk to the center of the room. On the middle of the desk they lighted a bunch of incense. Yingtai and Shanbo knelt down in front of the desk and bowed to the sky three times. When they stood up, Yingtai bowed to Shanbo.

"Brother Liang, now you have a younger brother."

"And now you have an older brother." Shanbo returned her bow.

Yinxin and Sijiu bowed to Shanbo and Yingtai respectively.

"From now on, we have a special bond between us. This bond is not created by bloodline. It is built upon all the things we share, especially the trust we have for each other. Whatever happens, we will always be there for each other," Shanbo said solemnly.

Sijiu said, "I was thinking...since our Masters have become brothers, Yinxin and I should become sworn brothers too. Neither of us have any family here. I would like to have a brother too."

"Me, too," Yinxin agreed. She was blushing and winked at Yingtai.

Shanbo looked at Yingtai smilingly. "What would you say?"

"Look, the incense is still burning." Yingtai turned to Yinxin and Sijiu and said, "Why don't you undertake the ritual for yourselves now?"

"I am nineteen, that makes me the older brother, as Yinxin is only sixteen."

Yinxin and Sijiu went through the same process that Yingtai and Shanbo had undergone.

"Well, well, this is a very important occasion for us. We must have some wine at dinner to celebrate the occasion," Shanbo said with delight.

"I don't usually drink wine, but I will have one or two bowls today," Yingtai said.

Shanbo sent Sijiu for some wine and food while Yinxin went to set the table with four red candles. Before long the table was full of food. The cook made them roast chicken, steamed fish, shrimp, bean curd and vegetables.

When everything was ready, Yingtai poured wine for Shanbo and herself. Shanbo was a little restless with excitement, smiling from ear to ear. Yingtai had never seen him so happy. This alone filled her with incredible delight.

"Here, let us toast our brotherhood!" The four of them got up and raised their bowls. They clinked bowls. Shanbo held his head up and finished the wine in one go. Yingtai looked at

Yinxin, who gave her an encouraging look, took a sip tentatively, swallowed it, and made a face to herself.

"My dear brother, I know you don't drink. But this is a special occasion. You have to make an exception. You are supposed to finish your bowl like I did," Shanbo said to her challengingly.

Yingtai closed her eyes and forced the wine down. She had to keep her mouth open when the wine went down. The stream of liquid burned all the way down her throat. For a moment, she felt as if she had been seized by fire.

"That is wonderful!" Shanbo lost his usual reserve and patted Yingtai on the shoulder. He poured himself another bowl and filled Yingtai's as well.

"Brother Yingtai, I cannot tell you how happy I am. I never had any brothers. Now I have a dear younger brother. And we are studying together every day. What could be better?" Throwing his head back, he swallowed the second bowl in its entirety.

Yingtai fixed her eyes upon Shanbo, aware more than ever before that he was male, a real man, one very different from the man she had been pretending to be. He was the first man she had ever been so physically close to. And he looked so perfect to her. She knew Shanbo was happy because of their newly celebrated tie of brotherhood. Suddenly she felt overwhelmingly happy as well because she had a good reason, a legitimate reason, to be really close to him.

"Hey, brother, you are not drinking!" Seeing that Yingtai's bowl was still full, Shanbo urged her to drink.

"I told you I am not a good drinker. I have reached my limit," Yingtai said with reservation.

"Oh, come on. You can allow yourself to go a little crazy just for this day. If worse comes to worst, you will only get a bit drunk. Then I will take care of you." Shanbo poured himself another bowl as he said this. He raised the bowl.

Yingtai knew she could not refuse him. "All right, I think I can handle another half bowl. But that will be all I can do tonight. Then I will watch you drink."

"Whatever your pleasure." Shanbo raised his bowl higher, making sure that Yingtai was ready to drink.

They then drank. Shanbo emptied the bowl, but Yingtai carefully measured the amount she took to make sure she was not drinking too much.

Feeling a little dizzy, Yingtai helped herself to some food. Shanbo was now ready for the fourth bowl. "After this, you can take the wine away," he said to Sijiu.

Yinxin noticed that Yingtai's face was all red and her eyes were a bit misty. "Are you all right?" she asked in a low voice. "Have some tea. I hear it can dilute the wine."

"Not quite, my heart is beating like a wild animal. But I think I can hold on for a while. Yes, I would like some tea," Yingtai said with a little difficulty, her mind spacing out. "I don't want to spoil Shanbo's evening."

Shanbo took some food and happened to see Yingtai resisting a yawn. "Yingtai, are you all right? It looks you did drink a little too much," he said in a concerned voice.

"I think I will be fine. I am just feeling a little sleepy. I had better lie down for a while." Yingtai got up to walk, but seemed to miss a step. She steadied herself by leaning against the table.

Shanbo stepped forward, putting his right arm around her shoulder. "Let me help you to bed."

Yingtai stiffened. She was not supposed to have any physical contact with a man. Dizzy as she was, she knew she could not tell him the truth. That would mean the end of her study there. But how was she going to stop his intimate assistance?

Yingtai was motionless, not knowing what to do.

"You are drunk. I can see that. You will be all right after some sleep. Come on, let me help you." Holding her closer, Shanbo was almost carrying her.

Yingtai's hair touched his face. She could even feel his chin where the little beard had grown at the end of the day. She could smell him and he smelt good. Yingtai became very alert, overwhelmed by a strong yet strange feeling that was unknown to her. All her strength left her. She set herself free and let him handle her body. She dropped to bed as soon as she was near enough to it, grateful that Shanbo had let go of her.

Shanbo helped Yinxin to take off Yingtai's shoes. Yingtai rolled to the other side of the bed fully clad. Shanbo told Yinxin to step aside because he wanted to take care of his brother at such a time. He leaned forward to the single bed, trying to unbutton Yingtai's clothes.

"This is strange. You are wearing a shirt instead of a vest under your clothes. And how come your shirt has all these buttons, from the sleeve to the chest?" Shanbo asked.

Yingtai was so frightened that she instantly awoke from her stupor. She became aware that he was undressing her! She had bound her breasts tightly, but happened to be wearing woman's clothes underneath her outer garments. Now how could she explain this to him? What story could she possibly concoct? Her mind raced as she tried to come up with something.

"Oh, there is a good reason for that. My mother has not been enjoying good health. I heard from a fortune-teller that if I wore a shirt underneath my clothing, one with a lot of buttons, she would be a healthy person within a few years. I don't really believe this, but you never know. So I do this for my mother, just in case."

"It sounds superstitious. But it is a nice thing for you to do."

"I know. I have gotten used to wearing it anyway. That is why I keep it on, just on the off-chance that the fortune-teller is right."

This explanation satisfied Shanbo. He tucked her in. "Sleep well, my good brother. You will be all right in the morning. If you need anything, you know where I am. Good night." Patting her on the shoulder, he left.

Yingtai heard him tell Sijiu and Yinxin to clean up in a low voice. Soon everything quieted down. "He is such a nice man." She thought to herself. She could still feel the warmth of his arm on her shoulder. With that, she felt fast asleep.

It was broad daylight when Yingtai woke up the next morning. The sky had cleared up and the bamboo leaves were dancing in the breeze. Yingtai startled: it must be very late.

"Shanbo! Are you there?"

"Yes, I am here. Yinxin has been here twice. You were sleeping soundly, so I sent him back to his room. Let me tell him that you are up."

Yinxin soon came to help Yingtai with washing and dressing.

"I hope I did not make much noise last night." Yingtai went into Shanbo's room. He was practicing calligraphy at the desk.

"No, you slept like a log. I called your name several times to check on you. You never answered me." Shanbo raised his head from his writing.

Yingtai looked at the characters he wrote. "Shanbo, your calligraphy is much better than mine. I had better give it some practice."

"But you must not write the way I do. They say my calligraphy is good, but they can tell from the way I write that I am a bookworm, whatever that means."

Yingtai laughed. "I love your calligraphy. But don't be offended if I tell you that you are indeed a bookworm in some ways."

"What do you mean?" Shanbo asked anxiously.

"I cannot tell you right now. Some day you will know," Yingtai said mysteriously.

"Why not tell me now?"

"Because the time is not right."

"Are you sure? I want to know it now."

"Trust me, you don't need to know it now. Sometimes it is good to have a little suspense in life," Yingtai insisted. "I promise I will tell you as soon as the time is right for you to know."

"You are making me very curious."

"Then I will simply change the subject. We should get things ready for our afternoon class."

Yingtai fled into her room. She was very tempted to tell him the truth and see how or if their relationship would change. But she could not afford to.

With summer coming, days got warmer. Yingtai and Yinxin used to wear thick and long-sleeved clothes for spring, but summer was making it impossible. They decided to wear at least two long-sleeved shirts to reduce the chance of revealing their female figures.

One hot evening Yingtai and Shanbo were reading by the same candle as usual. Shanbo saw Yingtai fanning herself.

"We are not going out anywhere tonight. Why not take off your gown?" he asked.

"Oh, I am used to this. Besides, this big shady room feels cool most of the time. I have always been weaker than others. If I wear less, I might get a cold. That would be worse." Yingtai struggled to find a reason to explain her eccentric way of dressing, but her lame excuse did not sound convincing even to herself. She looked at Shanbo helplessly, hoping he would just accept what she said.

Shanbo was not convinced, but he chose to let the bookworm take over him. He did not question Yingtai further.

"Well, Yingtai, you have to admit that some of your ways are a bit unusual." He secretly laughed at Yingtai and thought to himself: he says that I am a bookworm, but when it comes to clothing, he is a bit of a bookworm himself.

One day Yinxin came to Yingtai's room while Shanbo was not in.

"Shall we go for a walk? Master Zhou lives near here. You have said that Mrs. Zhou is a very nice person. We might bump into her and borrow some needle and thread from her. Some of your clothes need mending."

Yingtai was feeling bored without Shanbo in the next room, so was happy to go out. They walked to the back of the house where there was a path leading up to the higher part of the mountain. They followed it until they reached one of the peaks.

"What a view!" exclaimed Yingtai. They were overlooking scenery that she never dreamed of seeing in the small world she used to live in: patches of land, scattered houses, lakes here and there and grass and trees all around. Nature seemed to have casually mixed all of this together. It looked more beautiful than any human creation. Yingtai opened her eyes wide and took a deep breath as if this could help her take in everything she saw.

"Coming to Hangzhou was the best decision in my life. I could have never imagined that there is such beauty in the world locked away in my little study." Yingtai said with a faraway look in her eyes. Yinxin did not say a word. She knew Yingtai was communicating with herself.

"How unfair it is that most women cannot even go out of the house and never have a chance to see nature. And they are not even allowed to learn to read, so they cannot even use their imagination to dream what the world is like outside their home."

"I am so fortunate that I learned along with my brothers. I am so blessed that I managed to talk my parents into letting me come to Hangzhou. I am so lucky that I have Shanbo studying with me." Yingtai's face shone as she mentioned Shanbo's name.

"I think you like Master Liang very much." Yinxin commented with a smile that made Yingtai feel she was being seen clear through.

"Of course I like him. He is my brother."

"But you know you are a woman and he is a man. And he thinks you are his brother, not his sister."

"So?" Yingtai was getting upset. Yinxin knew it was time to shut up.

Yingtai felt depressed all of a sudden. The more she liked Shanbo, the guiltier she felt. She wanted him to know the truth, but was not sure how he would react to it. That could well bring to an end the way they had been living. Even if they liked each other as a man and a woman, what could come out of it? A single man and a single woman were not supposed to get to know each other without getting married first. No one would recognize their relationship.

"Let us go back," said Yingtai in low spirit.

They walked downhill quietly. As they were getting near home, they saw a woman washing vegetables by a well.

"That must be Mrs. Zhou," Yinxin said. "Let's go and talk with her."

Yingtai had met Mrs. Zhou once on a formal visit to Master Zhou's house with Shanbo. She greeted Mrs. Zhou and bowed, "How are you, Mrs. Zhou?"

"Fine, thank you. I have not seen you for a long time, Yingtai. How is everything?"

"Everything is going very well. I am learning a lot from Master Zhou." Turning to Yinxin, she said, "this is Yinxin, my helper and friend since childhood."

Yinxin stepped forward and bowed to Mrs. Zhou.

Mrs. Zhou nodded. She looked at both of them observantly. "Yingtai, you must have experienced some inconveniences living away from home like this ..."

"Oh, yes ..." Yinxin could not help interrupting.

"But Master Zhou has taken very good care of us." Yingtai interrupted her, fearing that she would say things that might reveal their secret.

Mrs. Zhou smiled understandingly. "If you need to borrow anything, feel free to come to me."

"Right now, we do need to find some needle and thread. May we borrow some from you?" Yingtai asked.

"Sure," said Mrs. Zhou, "but these are usually for women. You know how to use them?"

Yinxin was about to say something when Yingtai said, "Men in our village can do some simple needlework. They go out to work a lot. This helps a lot when they are not home."

"So you know a little needlework too?" asked Mrs. Zhou.

"I guess I can manage better than some women," Yingtai said, laughing.

Mrs. Zhou laughed too. Turning to Yinxin, she said, "You can come to my house to get the things you need a little later."

Yingtai began to worry. Mrs. Zhou seemed to have sensed something unusual about them. She warned Yinxin to be careful with what she would say when seeing Mrs. Zhou again.

CHAPTER 6

BEFORE LONG, IT would be July Seventh. According to the Chinese lunar calendar, as folklore had it, July Seventh was the day when two lovers from two different stars met in the Milky Way. It was said that the two lovers, the Herd-boy and the Weaving-girl, had been separated by force and could only meet once a year on the evening of July Seventh.

It was a calm evening. The Milky Way spanned across the sky and a half moon was hanging low, leaving very clear shadows on the earth. Yingtai was half lying on a folding chair, looking up into the sky, deep in thought.

Shanbo asked in a raised voice in his room, "Yingtai, where are you?"

"I am in the yard. It is nice and cool here. Would you like to come out? We can talk for a while."

"All right," Shanbo came out with a stool, placing it near Yingtai's chair.

"It is July Seventh. I guess we should take it easy this evening."

"You know about July Seventh?"

"Of course I do. I also know what people do on this day. In my village young women lay fruits in the yard. If spiders come and make webs around the fruits, that means the coming year will bring a good harvest for fruits."

"You are partly right about that tradition, but you have not mentioned the rest of the belief within that tradition."

"What is that?"

Yingtai sat up. "It also means that the young woman who lays out the fruit will be ensured of finding a nice husband during the coming year. Do your people believe the same in your village?"

"Oh yes, now I remember. You are absolutely correct. Have you ever watched the girls perform that act?"

"No, not really. I have heard that they have to prepare five different color scarves and tie them onto the fruits."

"That is interesting. But do you think, like I do, that the story of the Herd-boy and the Weaving-girl is a bit ludicrous? Imagine! The Weaving-girl had to lose the Herd-boy simply because her weaving was not good enough. Her punishment for this transgression was that she could only see the Herd-boy once a year on July Seventh. A rather severe punishment, right?" Shanbo queried.

Yingtai was quiet for a while. She looked at the sky, sighed and said, "The Milky Way is so wide. How can the two see each other every day across it without being able to meet? This punishment is beyond human endurance. But then again, miserable things like this can happen on earth too. Some people don't even get to meet even once a year."

Shanbo looked at the sky. The moon had gone and the Milky Way was still there with bright stars around it. "Perhaps the Weaving-girl and the Herd-boy are meeting right now. Like you said, they can at least meet once a year, but there are people on earth that simply cannot meet this often."

Yingtai missed a heartbeat at this. They had come to a sensitive topic. She had never exchanged anything of an emotional nature with Shanbo. She tried to calm herself and kept still in the chair. "Do you know of such people?"

"Well, for example, the gatekeeper here at school. He told me that he has not been home for over two years. It is difficult to imagine how his wife is taking it."

"I was thinking, what if a sculptor made two sculptures, one of a man and one of a woman. He had not intended them as husband and wife, but the statues somehow made themselves a couple. Then what if the sculptor learned of this and became angry with them. As punishment, he placed one of them in the front yard and the other in the backyard so that they would never meet again. That would be the most tragic." Yingtai sounded extremely sad as she finished.

"Ha ha ha ..." Shanbo laughed. "You sound so silly. You are like a three-year-old. Sculptures are sculptures. They don't have a life. How can they be a couple? You are not making any sense."

Yingtai laughed too. "Am I not making much sense? Let me try to make more sense. You can at least tell which is a male sculpture and which is a female sculpture. They can still pass as a couple, though not a real one. However, sometimes you cannot tell whether a person is a man or woman. In that case, it is worse than the sculpture couple."

"Ha ha! You are not making any more sense than before. Yingtai, you sound a bit off tonight. We have to get up early tomorrow. I think you are over tired. You had better go to bed now." Shanbo assumed his role of a big brother.

"I feel like staying here a little longer. You go ahead and I will go in soon." The conversation sank Yingtai into a very disturbed mood. She decided she had to be alone to calm down.

"Are you sure you don't want me to stay with you?"

"Yes, I am sure. Good night."

Shanbo got up, stretched himself and slowly went to his room. He smiled to himself when he thought of what Yingtai had just said, amused that he could think of such strange and fanciful things to say.

Yingtai's eyes followed him all the way. She did not know at which point she had begun to experience a feeling of both happiness and sadness whenever she looked at him. She was agonized by some kind of expectation, but something beyond her control always hung over her, making her fear that her relationship with Shanbo could be destroyed at any time. Worse still, she knew she could not afford it to happen.

Yingtai drifted into sleep in spite of the disturbing thoughts. When she woke up, she felt something heavy landing on her. It was Shanbo putting a blanket over her!

"I am sorry I woke you up. It was getting chilly," Shanbo apologized.

"Oh, it is so wonderful to have a brother like you," Yingtai said. She felt something special inside herself. She had never had any man showing her any concern like this. She had thought that only women knew how to take care of others this way. "I never want to be separated from you, Shanbo," she said.

Shanbo smiled, "Well, some day we have to go home, but we will still be brothers. We will visit each other a lot. I don't want you to be out of my life either."

"Promise me that we will try to find a way to be very close together." Yingtai felt worried as if they would have to say good-bye tomorrow.

"I promise." He looked at her with brotherly affection. He thought to himself that Yingtai was sometimes very vulnerable and this made him want to protect him.

The next day when Yingtai and Shanbo came back from their class, Yinxin was waiting for them in their apartment, with a basket of fruit on the table.

"These are from last night. They were the offerings to the Herd-boy and the Weaving-girl."

"Were you doing the girl thing yesterday with the fruit? Were you hoping to get a wife this year?" Shanbo asked jokingly.

"I don't think I need to do that. Our spouses are almost here for us, are they not, Master?" Yinxin said, turning to Yingtai.

Yingtai sat down at the table. "Go away! That is not a good joke." Laughing, she waved Yinxin out of the room.

"Neither of you know what you are talking about when you joke. I don't get it." Shanbo was more puzzled than amused.

Yingtai and Yinxin looked at each other and burst into laughter, Yingtai bending down and Yinxin wiping tears.

"You have to get to know us in the Zhu Village to understand us," Yinxin said in between laughter.

"Stop right there, Yinxin," Yingtai warned. "You are confusing Master Liang."

Shanbo did not laugh. He observed. "There is something strange about both of you, but I just cannot put my finger on what it is. You have definitely sounded odder these past two days."

"Well, well. Don't be silly, Shanbo. Are we not all special and strange individuals?" Yingtai stopped laughing and collected herself. "Come on now, let us be serious. How about practicing our calligraphy?"

Two more months went by. Master Zhou gave the students a one-day holiday for the Double Ninth Festival, a traditional day to show respect for the old and for outdoor activities. The evening before that day, Yingtai and Shanbo were studying together as usual.

At some point, Yingtai took her eyes off the book and asked, "What are we going to do tomorrow? Shall we go somewhere for fun?"

"That is up to you. If you prefer to stay at home reading, I will stay here with you."

"I want to go out. We don't have many holidays here. I think Yinxin and Sijiu are pretty bored staying around here all the time. They have been looking forward to this day. They will be disappointed if we don't go anywhere."

"Then we'll go somewhere. I hear that the West Lake is nice. It is a shame that we have not been there yet. Everyone says that it is the best Hangzhou has to offer."

"You must be reading my mind! I have read and heard a lot about it too. They say that its beauty lies not only in the lake itself, but also in the surrounding area which is untouched wilderness."

"Mm, I think we can have a good time there. I will have Sijiu get prepared right away. What do you say to a picnic on the lake tomorrow?"

"It is great that you want to go. I will make sure that Yinxin and Sijiu get everything ready." Yingtai was overjoyed.

It was a bright morning, sunny and cool, with a soft breeze. Yingtai and Shanbo walked down the mountain. Yinxin and Sijiu followed, carrying food and drinks. It was an hour-long hike on foot.

Shanbo and Yingtai had been down the mountain only a few times. There was not much entertainment provided for the students at the time. As a result, any trip could make Yingtai excited. She had a hard time trying not to make everyone stop to observe things that were usually of interest only to women. She knew that being out in nature never failed to energize her.

They could smell the lake a long way away. Soon they were able to see the willow trees and their reflections upon the lake. They could see some tourists around the lake. However, in comparison to the size of the lake, the number of people was very small. Each group of people had plenty of space to themselves.

They walked along the lake for a while, admiring the work of Nature: there was nothing else there except the water, the reflections of nearby trees and hills in the water. The ripples changed the reflections constantly, breaking them and giving the lake new patterns.

"This is a wonderful place, though it could be better if there were some benches and pavilions at intervals. Then people could walk around and take breaks when they chose to," Shanbo commented.

"There will be someday, I am sure. The breeze is so soothing here," Yingtai said. She paused and said again, "I wish we could be young forever. So we would never have to leave school. I can honestly say that this has been the best time of my life. I am surely going to miss these days when they are gone."

"Why are you so pessimistic, Yingtai? You will have a great future after you finish school. Your good days are yet to come," Shanbo said.

"No, you don't know the truth." These words came out from Yingtai before she realized.

"What truth?" Shanbo became very concerned. "How bad is the truth?"

Yingtai's heart almost stop beating. "The truth, the truth is that I, well, I mean, my father wants me to ... to take care of things at home," she stammered, "which means that I will be confined to the house and will not be able to use what I have learned here."

"But I am sure you will still go out a lot and get involved with many things in and outside the village," Shanbo argued.

"Well, I certainly hope that you are correct, Shanbo." Yingtai thought it a good idea to drop the topic before Shanbo got suspicious. "Anyway, we should change the topic. Enough about the future—we are here today to have fun!"

"Absolutely." Shanbo responded, trying to steady himself on the irregular pebbles and stones as he walked. Almost instinctively, he came close to Yingtai and held her every so often to make sure she was walking steadily.

Neither of them spoke any further. There was only the sound of their footsteps on the stones. For Yingtai, the silence was close to sweet torture. She could not bear to be so close to Shanbo without sharing her most relevant feelings with him. She was secretly happy to be able to enjoy the freedom of being close, almost intimate with a man she liked, which was something totally undreamed of for women of her time. But it was frustrating not to be able to reveal it to anyone and to live in fear that if Shanbo knew her identity. She suspected that she was in love with Shanbo, but what could she do with this love? Man and woman were not supposed to seek love without a go-between and parental consent. She could not bring herself to imagine what her relationship with Shanbo would be when they finished their program of study.

Yingtai enjoyed being in such close physical contact with Shanbo. It felt warm and secure. But she wanted him to know she had these feelings as a woman, not as a brother. She was aware that she should try to keep her distance from Shanbo whenever she could manage to. But how could she, as a brother, recoil from his touch without hurting or puzzling Shanbo?

"There are some boats over there. We can rent one and go onto the lake." Shanbo broke the silence. "It would be relaxing to view the countryside from the lake."

"What a good idea!" Yingtai was relieved.

Sijiu went to rent a boat.

It was a very small boat. After Yingtai and Shanbo had got into it, Yinxin and Sijiu had to squeeze in at the bow. The boatman steered at the rear.

The boat moved slowly. The mountains and hills around the lake came in and out of view. Willow branches occasionally drifted by, hitting the boat gently. Shanbo put his hand into the water and scooped up one branch.

"When we first met, the willow trees were just showing their leaves. Now it looks the leaves are soon to fall. How time flies!" Shanbo said thoughtfully.

"I wish we had a way to stop time, so we could be gliding along like this for the rest of our lives," Yingtai said with a touch of sadness in her voice.

"I wish it were possible too," said Shanbo.

"Since it is not possible, you should go crazy and enjoy yourself now," Yinxin said.

"Yes, let us have some wine," Sijiu said. "We will not stop until we all get drunk."

"Don't be silly. How can we get back?" Yinxin asked.

"Yinxin is right. We should enjoy ourselves, but we had better not get drunk," said Shanbo.

They got off the boat and sat down under some willow trees. Yinxin made two shares of wine and food, one for Yingtai and Shanbo and the other for Sijiu and herself.

Shanbo held Yingtai's hand in his. "This is the first major festival I have spent away from home. But I feel at home because of you." He raised the wine bowl and continued, "Let us drink to our brotherhood." Swallowing more than half of the bowl, he gave the rest to Yingtai.

Filled with happiness, Yingtai took over the bowl and drank. She had not shared wine from the same bowl with Shanbo before and she could hardly handle the intimacy of drinking from it. Strangely enough, the wine did not burn as it did the first time and she felt warm and excited as the wine went down her throat.

"Will we be together this time next year?" she asked. Their hands were still joined and she was hoping that Shanbo would not take his back.

"We will be. And the year after that too, and more, I hope." Apparently Shanbo was saying that because the scheduled time for Master Zhou's program was three years.

But Yingtai was very pleased that he wanted to spend many more such occasions with her. She smiled. It was almost like hearing Shanbo promise her something for their future.

CHAPTER 7

BY THE END of their first year at school, Yingtai and
Shanbo got to know most of their classmates well. They
would invite the new friends to their apartment once in a
while. Obviously, no other two students were in a closer
relationship than they were. Consequently they often became
the talking stock among classmates. Shanbo was known as
intelligent yet a bit bookish, Yingtai as intelligent and witty.
Everyone noticed that Yingtai did not look manly enough,
some had even commented that Yingtai was in some ways
like a woman. But no one ever suspected anything since
Yingtai's trick was unheard of in the history of education.

One day Yingtai went out for a walk alone when Shanbo
was called away by Master Zhou. When she came back,
Yingtai found Shanbo sitting with his arms round his knees,
staring into the sky.

"Is there anything wrong?" Yingtai could tell that something was bothering him.

"I am feeling very depressed. But I don't want to talk
about it." Shanbo did not look at Yingtai.

Yingtai never saw him so distressed. For a while, she did
not know what to do. "Is it something I said or I did?" she
asked timidly.

"No, it has nothing to do with you. You are a great brother."

"Then it must have to do with Master Zhou. Was he unhappy with what you wrote yesterday?"

"No, even if he was, I would be happy because that is the way to learn."

"Then what is it? Oh, I know, you must be homesick."

"Well, not quite. My parents are fine. But you are right to some extent."

"Are you saying that they miss you?"

Shanbo sighed. "I might as well tell you the truth. I just got a letter from home. My father asked me to go home because they have run out of money and can no longer support my education."

"So are you going home?" Yingtai suddenly became nervous.

"I have to." Shanbo said as he looked at Yingtai and held her hands, "I can handle leaving school. I think I can study at home. But how can I leave you like this after all the time we have spent and all the things we have done together?"

"How can you go home now? You had a good start here. You have a brother here too," Yingtai said almost accusingly.

"I know, I know. But what can I do? I cannot afford to stay here," Shanbo said desperately. "Can't you see that is why I am so sad?"

"Are you sure money is the only reason you have to go home?"

"Yes." Shanbo looked away from her.

Yingtai held his hands tight. She saw some hope.

"Then you can stay. My parents will keep sending me money. I received more than I could spend last year and have some savings. You can share things with me and I will spend less on unnecessary items. I am sure we will have enough to get by." She was getting excited as she said this, her hands holding him tighter as if he would go away if she let go.

"Thank you for the offer. But I simply cannot accept it."

"Why not? Are we not brothers?" Yingtai was getting upset.

"Of course we are brothers. But ..."

"But what? You are going to stay. That is all there is to it."

"It is your parents' money. They may not like the idea."

"I am not asking them to send me extra money. We will just share what they send me. Is that good enough?"

Shanbo was going to say something before Yingtai stopped him. "If you leave, I will probably have to go back too. I know I will not do well here without you."

Seeing that Yingtai was very firm, Shanbo agreed to her arrangement.

"All right. I will write and tell my parents," he conceded.

From that point on, Shanbo studied even harder than before. Yingtai did the same, hoping that this would get her more of Shanbo's respect and attention.

One evening both were reading by the desk. Shanbo noticed that Yingtai was dozing off.

"Yingtai, you look tired. Perhaps you should go to bed early tonight," he suggested.

"Maybe I should. I feel tired. In fact I have not been quite myself since this morning." Rising, Yingtai made for her room. But her strength seemed to have left her and she could hardly move.

"Yinxin, come and help me," she said mechanically.

Shanbo became worried. "Are you sick?"

"I have a headache and I ache all over." Yingtai did not want to alarm him. "I am sure I will be all right if I sleep for the next day or two."

Shanbo got up and came after them. Yinxin took care not to let him see Yingtai when she helped her undress, then covered her from shoulder to heel.

"I will get a doctor first thing tomorrow morning." Shanbo felt Yingtai's forehead. "My, you are burning hot! I will go and get the doctor right now!"

"No! Please don't bother! I know myself. I will be better soon enough. I must have gotten a cold last night. It is really not so serious."

"In that case, let Yinxin go back to his room. I will look after you tonight."

"No, you have to go to class tomorrow. Yinxin does not have anything to do anyway. He can sleep in the folding chair next to my bed. If I need anything, I can wake him up."

"Yes, I will take good care of Master Zhu."

Shanbo was getting very upset. "Yingtai, sometimes you are just too stubborn. Do you realize how ill you are? I want to be here for you. I insist. I will sleep right next to you."

"You will not sleep well that way." Yingtai did not dare to reject him any more for fear of making him suspicious.

"It will be the best way. I don't think I will sleep well anywhere else. I must make sure I am here when you need me." Shanbo was very firm.

Yingtai did not know what to say. She knew him well. When he wanted to do something, he would do it and he would do it well.

Yinxin was worried: he might discover her secret! But what could she say to change his mind without causing him to suspect anything?

"Master Liang, I am here to serve Master Zhu. I should be here tonight."

"I know. But you might not wake up when he calls for you. You cannot change my mind. I will be sharing the bed with Yingtai tonight. You may go now."

Yingtai knew Shanbo would not change his mind. "All right, Yinxin, you'd better leave. I will call you if I need you badly enough. Don't worry. I will be fine," she assured her.

Yinxin nodded, her eyes full of concern.

"I will be all right. You can make some tea for me before you go."

Yingtai turned around to the wall side of the bed after sipping some tea.

She soon fell asleep.

She woke up in the middle of the night. The candle was still burning. She turned to find Shanbo reading at her bed-side. Shanbo shifted his eyes from the book and met her eyes. "Are you feeling better?"

"Not too bad, but not much better either."

Shanbo put the book down to feel her forehead. "Your fever is still very high. Are you sure you don't want me to get a doctor?"

"Yes. I want to wait till tomorrow. Could you call Yinxin for me?"

"What for?"

Yingtai went quiet, her eyes fixing on the mosquito net.

"What is it that you cannot talk to me about?"

An embarrassed look came to Yingtai's eyes. She struggled with herself for a while and said, "I guess it is all right to tell you. I need to use the bathroom."

"You don't need Yinxin for this. I will help you up and go to the bathroom with you."

Yingtai sat up panting a little. "When I was little, my father told me that going to the bathroom is a private thing and one should go alone. I know I will be more comfortable if Yinxin is here to help. And he will be just waiting for me outside the bathroom." She looked up to Shanbo who was bending over her. "It is good enough that you are here for me. Yinxin can do the job. Besides, I want you to continue with your reading."

Shanbo was not very convinced but thought Yingtai had a point. He called Yinxin who came right away. Yinxin held Yingtai and supported her all the way to the bathroom which was only a few steps away from the room. When they were back, Yingtai was too weak to move another step. She threw herself to bed, gasping for air.

Shanbo was anxious about her situation. "Yingtai, you are getting weaker. Don't attempt to do this any more. I will bring a bucket in here."

Yingtai agreed. Shanbo tucked her in and asked Yinxin to leave. "I will call you if needed."

Yinxin nodded, but did not move. She was looking at Yingtai. On her face was the unasked question: "are you going to be all right?"

"Please go, Yinxin," Yingtai said.

"Sleep well, Master Zhu," Yinxin said as she left.

"Shanbo, it is late. You must go off to bed too."

"I will. But I am not going anywhere. I will sleep right next to you."

"I think you will be better off sleeping in your own room. I promise I will call you if I need help."

"No, you are not going to change my mind. How can I leave you when you have such a high fever? If you don't want me to find a doctor, you have to let me be at your side."

Yingtai was speechless. They had been acting like brothers. Rejecting him now would seem odd, but letting him sleep next to herself would be most inappropriate. What if he found out she was a woman?

On the other hand, she had come to believe that she would not take anyone as her husband except Shanbo, though she did not know how that was going to happen yet. Even so, she was not supposed to sleep with him like this before marriage. They were not even engaged. No, he did not have the slightest idea that she was a woman. Tortured by all these thoughts, Yingtai twisted herself constantly in bed.

"Yingtai, tell me what is bothering you?"

"I understand and appreciate why you want to stay with me, but I ..."

"But what? But you are a patient? Are you afraid that you will pass your cold onto me?" Shanbo sat on the bed. "Listen, I don't care. All I care is that you will be safe tonight."

Yingtai said she understood. "But I want you to know one thing. I have been very much spoiled at home. I have always slept on my own. I am worried that I will not be able to sleep if you are next to me."

Shanbo looked frustrated.

"Perhaps we can do this. In fact I have done this at home a few times with my mother. It was like a game. We would put bowls of water between the two of us. That would keep us away from each other. Whoever went over the line and spilled the water would get punished. Since we are brothers, we could do the same thing. What do you think?"

Shanbo was relieved and excited. "I will do whatever you did with your mother. But what would be the punishment?"

"The loser will treat the winner to dinner at a restaurant."

Now Shanbo started to get suspicious. "You must be kidding."

"No, honestly, you can ask Yinxin. He has been in restaurants with me several times. It may sound stupid, but we did that for fun. And I did this only with my mother."

"All right. Let us keep the tradition then, though it is a bad time to play the game," Shanbo said. "But I suggest that we don't use water. I don't want you to get wet. That would not help you recover."

Shanbo rose and got out the two bowls they used for meals. "No, they are not enough. Get some more," Yingtai said. Strangely she felt better after inventing the ridiculous story and seeing Shanbo willing to put it into practice.

Shanbo shook his head in his good-natured way, went to his room and came back with three more bowls. "Will these be enough?"

Yingtai could not believe that Shanbo took the whole thing so seriously.

She was hoping that he would get discouraged enough to give up the idea. But he simply took everything she said seriously. No wonder people had said that he was a bookworm. But somehow she liked his bookwormish ways.

She did not like men that were too shrewd. She had read a lot of stories about how bad men could be. But Shanbo was different. He was definitely reliable, though a bit too naive sometimes.

Yingtai nodded, trying to repress a laugh.

"Now what else do we need?" Shanbo asked, failing to notice Yingtai's amused look.

Yingtai could hardly keep herself from laughing. "Just a blanket."

At long last, Shanbo lay down next to the row of bowls parallel to Yingtai.

"You are my best brother, Shanbo," Yingtai said, giving his hand an emotional grip across the bowls.

"You are my best and only brother, Yingtai." Shanbo said with equal feeling.

Yingtai could not trust herself to say anything else. "Shall we try to get some sleep?" she suggested and turned to the other side of the bed, giving Shanbo her back.

Shanbo thought that she was exhausted by all the talk and the fuss of getting the bowls ready. He was tired too. But he wanted to make sure that Yingtai was asleep before he fell asleep. He waited for about ten minutes and decided that she was asleep. Then he leaned over and felt Yingtai's palm. Her fever seemed to have gone down a lot. He saw that her face was not as red as before. Relieved, he blew out the candle. He let out a yawn and turned to the other side, taking care not to make any noise. He fell fast asleep right away.

Yingtai was wide awake. She pretended to be asleep because she wanted to avoid talking with Shanbo in such an intimate setting. When Shanbo felt her palm, she was tempted to respond but fought back the urge. She thought he would feel her forehead. Would he touch her face by mistake in the dark? How would that feel? For a moment, she was tense with fear and expectation. But Shanbo's hand did not come.

Yingtai was disappointed. In the meantime, she was filled with respect and admiration for Shanbo. Only the good-natured and simple-honest-minded Shanbo would have done all this for her without questioning why she was behaving so strangely. She could not imagine who else would have accepted this trick as blindly as Shanbo had.

But suppose he had found out that she was a woman. Would he be still sleeping with her like this? Would he still touch her like he just did? Would he flee from the room or would he come closer to her? Realizing that her imagination had run wild, Yingtai was terrified and felt ashamed of herself.

But it was good enough to be lying so near him and to listen to his manly snores.

She did not go to sleep until it was nearly morning.

Yinxin came to the room twice, only to find that both Yingtai and Shanbo were still asleep. She was amused to find the line of bowls between them. Yingtai's arm was out of the blanket. Her skin was fine and fair. Anyone could tell that it was a woman's arm. But Shanbo was not anyone. He would be the last person in the world to notice.

Yingtai woke up the second time when Yinxin was there. They shared a quiet laugh looking at the row of bowls. Yingtai signaled that she wanted to go to the bathroom. Yinxin helped her out of bed very carefully.

When they came back, Shanbo startled and woke up.

"How are you feeling now?" he asked.

"I think I am better."

"But we still need a doctor to make sure you are going to be fine."

Yingtai agreed. Shanbo went out immediately.

A doctor of Chinese medicine came back with Shanbo within half an hour. He felt Yingtai's pulse and concluded that she had a cold. He gave Shanbo some advice about how to take care of her so that she would not suffer any complications. He prescribed some Chinese herbs and pronounced that she would recover in a few days.

That morning Sijiu went down the mountain to Hangzhou. He came back with a bucket after lunch time. Placing it near Yingtai's bed, he said, "Now you don't have to go into the bathroom any more. Yinxin will clean it for you often."

Yingtai tried not to show that she did not like the idea, and thanked him.

For the next four nights, Shanbo slept next to Yingtai with the bowls between them. Yingtai was extremely careful with everything she said and did. She used the bucket only when she was alone in the room. Shanbo did not seem to find anything unusual.

On the seventh day, Yingtai fully recovered. On the way to school that morning, Yingtai thanked Shanbo again.

"I don't know how to thank you more. For these many days, you have taken such good care of me, decocting the herbs, feeding me the liquid and everything. Even my parents could not have done better."

"But that was the only way to get the medicine into you. You were too weak to sit up and the liquid was getting cold."

"I remember your holding my head up and feeding the liquid into my mouth. Shanbo, only you would do this for me." Yingtai looked at Shanbo gratefully and meaningfully, wishing he knew what she was trying to convey.

"That is when you need a brother. I am glad I was there for you."

"I also remember that you fed me three meals, one spoonful after another. My brothers at home never did that for me, you know," Yingtai continued. She was trying hard to let Shanbo understand that their brotherhood was very special.

"I have never done this for anyone else either," said Shanbo, "but you did something special for me too."

Yingtai thought for a while and could not fathom what it could be. "What was it?"

"You said you only slept with your mother. So I was only the second person you ever slept with. I was very moved by that."

"Oh, yes. Those were very, very special times." Yingtai spoke out each word slowly. But she could not afford any more comments than that.

Yingtai and Shanbo's brotherhood became closer and stronger after that episode. Yingtai was less reserved than before in showing her care for Shanbo. Whatever Shanbo needed, she would have it ready for him.

One day Shanbo and Yingtai were having their customary walk after dinner.

"If I had a brother at home and if he were as caring as you are, there is nothing else I would ask for in the world," Shanbo declared.

"But am I not your brother now? I will be your brother always."

"But you have a family. You will have to go home to your parents some day."

"Since we are brothers, we are not supposed to leave each other. I will be with you for the rest of my life," Yingtai said willfully.

"It is very nice of you to say that. But you sound like a three-year-old making a promise to someone without knowing what you are talking about." He gave Yingtai a somewhat sad look. "But I appreciate that. I know you mean it, but we must accept the fact that we cannot always be this way."

"Yes, we can!" Yingtai said again and she smiled mischievously.

Shanbo looked at her, shook his head and said nothing.

CHAPTER 8

TWO YEARS PASSED. One spring morning, Shanbo was practicing calligraphy while Yingtai made Chinese ink for him by rubbing an ink stick on an ink stone. She was too focused on the job to feel that some ink splashed onto her face. Shanbo happened to look up from his writing and saw the black spots on her face. He took out a handkerchief and came close to her face to wipe them off.

"Oh!" He gave out a surprised cry.

"What?" Yingtai asked.

"I was not aware that you had your ears pierced. I thought only women do this. How come you did it too?" Shanbo asked curiously.

For a moment Yingtai failed to come up with anything for this unexpected incident. "What is it again?" She pretended she did not hear him very well.

"Oh, I was wondering why you had your ears pierced."

"Oh, that!" Yingtai's mind was busy making up a story. "If you had not mentioned it, I would not even have remembered that this had happened to me." By now she had calmed down.

"I was very weak when I was born. My parents prayed for my good health. Somehow they got this idea of piercing my ears. That meant I symbolically became a girl. Therefore it would be easier to raise me. Well, I don't really understand the story myself." Yingtai realized that she was not making much sense and decided to be vague about it.

Shanbo had heard of more ridiculous stories than this before, so he did not ask any more questions. This was the first time Shanbo had come near to the truth. Yingtai felt insecure and became more careful about everything after that.

A few months passed by. Yingtai and Shanbo had been studying with Master Zhou for nearly three years.

One day Yingtai was taking it easy in the backyard. A young man came to her and bowed. It was Shun Wang, who had been coming regularly to deliver money and messages from home.

"Here you are again. Is everything fine at home? Did you bring me another letter?"

Shun Wang handed her a letter. "Mrs. Zhu has not been feeling very well these days. Mr. Zhu wants you to come home as soon as you can. The letter will tell you everything."

Yingtai tore the letter open anxiously. It was a brief note: her mother was sick and she was asked to come home right away. There was no mention of what was wrong.

"Do you have any idea what the matter is with my mother?"

"No, I only knew she has taken to her bed for the past few days."

Yingtai read the letter again. She remembered that one of the things she had promised to do before she left home was that she would return immediately if her mother ever got sick. Now that her mother was sick, she should lose no time in going home. Besides, she had been away for three years.

"I will tell Yinxin to pack right away. I believe we can leave tomorrow morning," said Yingtai as she was walking to her room. "You take the heavier luggage and leave this evening. Yinxin and I will leave tomorrow."

She sent for Yinxin to take Shun Wang to a place where he could get some rest. She went into Shanbo's room and saw him lost in a book. All of a sudden, she was seized by an acute pain: she would be leaving him very soon! She went quietly to Shanbo and stood by him for a while before disrupting his reading.

"Shanbo."

"Yingtai." Shanbo put the book down. "Is anything the matter?"

"I just want to confirm something with you. How long have we been here together?"

"Close to three years," answered Shanbo, puzzled. "What is going on? There must be a reason when you ask that question."

"I am afraid so. I just got a letter from home. My mother is sick. I need to go back to see her." She hesitated a little before she continued. "I have a feeling that she is not very sick. But I have been away for three years. I simply cannot refuse when they ask me to return. What do you think?"

"You are right. You should go home. Hopefully you ..." He stopped himself, laughing and looking into Yingtai's eyes.

"I am sorry I am leaving so unexpectedly. I am going to miss you so very much. When you finish school here, please come to see me after you return home. Will you do that?" Yingtai was almost begging him.

"I will. I will certainly come to see you as soon as I can. I will stay home for only a few days. Then I will come and see you." Shanbo could not promise enough. "When are you leaving?"

"Tomorrow morning."

"So soon?" Shanbo was totally unprepared for this. "Then, then I must accompany you for as far as I can."

"No, please don't. You have got to go to classes."

"If you are not here, there is not much point for me to stay here."

Sijiu ran in at this point. "Yinxin told me that Master Zhu is leaving tomorrow."

Shanbo nodded.

"Did you ask him to stay?"

"I cannot. His mother is sick. All I can do is to walk him back for half a day. You can come with me."

"Of course I will. I am sure Master Zhu and you have a lot to say to each other before you say good-bye." Yinxin had come into the room and was happy to hear Shanbo's decision.

"Yinxin, I am not very good at words. But I can certainly help carry the luggage for you," Sijiu said.

Yinxin nodded without a word.

Yingtai was too upset to think straight. She thought for a while. "I have to notify Master Zhou of my leaving and say good-bye to him. Yinxin, will you start packing? I will be back soon."

There was no time to make an appointment. Yingtai went straight to Master Zhou's home. Master Zhou was surprised to see her and welcomed her in.

"I am sorry to come unannounced. But I have something urgent to tell you," Yingtai apologized.

"Calm yourself and sit down please," Master Zhou said kindly.

"I got a message from home earlier today. My mother is sick. I am afraid I have to go home right away. I am here to say good-bye to you. I would like to thank you for your supervision and all your help during my study here." Yingtai bowed to Master Zhou as she said this.

"You are most welcome, my child. You have been a wonderful student. I think you are doing the right thing by going home. When are you leaving?"

"Tomorrow morning. I would like to say good-bye to Mrs. Zhou too. She has been very kind to me."

"Wait just a minute. I will tell her that you are here."

Mrs. Zhou came out to meet Yingtai. "I heard that you are going home tomorrow," she said.

"Yes. I want to thank you for your kindness. You have been very helpful to me."

"I was glad to."

"Yinxin also wanted to come to say good-bye. He always says that you are very kind," Yingtai added.

"The only thing I did was to lend you the needle and thread."

"But it was great help for us. Thank you again Mrs. Zhou, and good-bye."

But Yingtai did not move. There was desperate eagerness in her eyes.

"You seem to want to tell me something, Yingtai. Is there anything I can do to help?" observed Mrs. Zhou.

Yingtai suddenly looked very shy and guilty. She looked away, her hands playing with one corner of her clothes.

"There is something that I have long wanted to reveal to ... to people." For a while, she felt unsure of herself. "I wanted so much to come to Hangzhou to learn new things."

"Yes?" Mrs. Zhou waited patiently. She did not want to push Yingtai.

"Now that I am about to leave, it really does not matter any more. Let me tell you the truth." Yingtai took a deep breath and gathered up her courage. "Yinxin and I, we are not men. We are women." Seeing that Mrs. Zhou was not very shocked, she continued, "the only way for me to come here to study was to disguise myself as a man."

"You did well, though I suspected you were women the first time I saw you. But you have been very careful. Your performance was perfect. There is not a man here who even suspected that," said Mrs. Zhou. "You are very brave and extremely clever. You deserve a good education. I wish I had done the same thing myself when I was younger."

Yingtai felt relieved and validated at the same time. "I shall never regret doing this. I have learned so much from Master Zhou."

"Come here and sit down. Take your time and tell me how you want me to help."

"How do you know I want you to help?" Yingtai asked curiously.

"Yingtai, how could I not know? I am a woman myself, you know. You want me to talk with Shanbo, correct?" Mrs. Zhou said, smiling.

Yingtai's face went very red. "Shanbo does not have the slightest idea whom I truly am. And he has been such a wonderful brother."

Mrs. Zhou waited for her to go on.

"I felt increasingly guilty for hiding my secret from him."

"Did you try to tell him?"

"I always wanted to. But I was scared. I did not know what would happen if he knew. I ... I did not want to change our relationship. I knew that if there was no brotherhood between us, I would not have been able to spend time with him the way I did."

"So you want me to tell him for you?"

"Would you?" Yingtai looked up. She was almost in tears.

"Of course I will, my dear. Is there anything else you want me to tell him?"

Tears ran down from Yingtai's cheeks. "Tell him that he is more than a brother to me. After spending the past three years with him, I cannot imagine having any other man near me. I will wait at home for him to come and ask my father for my hand in marriage."

"I can do that too. Now, is there anything you want me to give to him?"

Yingtai reached into the inner pocket of her clothes and took out a small butterfly pendant made of jade.

"I wore it on my necklace for as long as I can remember. Please give this to him and tell him to take it with him when he comes to see my father. My father knows that I have a couple of jade like this."

Mrs. Zhou took the jade butterfly and gave it a careful look. "You can depend on me, Yingtai."

"Thank you so much," said Yingtai as she bowed. Mrs. Zhou went in to ask Master Zhou to come out. Yingtai bowed to them both several times and left.

Yingtai felt much better walking back. On entering the room, she saw that Shanbo had put her belongings aside.

"Good for you! We have shared almost everything for so long. I don't think I could tell what is yours and what is mine," she said.

"That is exactly how I feel. I just set aside the things you liked best."

"That is not fair. You like many of the same things. How can you give them all to me?" she said as she walked over to the pile of belongings. Among them were two little mandarin ducks made of bronze. She picked them up and said, "You love these more than I do. You should keep them."

"I love them because you love them. I have seen you looking at them lost in thought. I am sure you love them more than I do."

Yingtai stroked the beak and feathers of the ducks affectionately. Putting them together, she fondled them and said, "Do they remind you a little of us? Please keep them. When you miss me, you can fondle them. Maybe you will feel something."

Shanbo laughed. "If you insist, I will keep them. But your wording was not very appropriate."

Yingtai knew that Shanbo would be aware that it was not an appropriate thing to say. She just wanted to at least arouse his suspicion before she left. But she simply could not count on Shanbo for he was so innocent and guileless. Unwilling to give up, she searched harder for provocative things to say. She spread out the things from the basket that Shanbo had packed for her. She noticed a pen container made of china. On it was drawn a pomegranate.

"Hey, why did you give this to me?"

"Is that not obvious enough? You come from a big family. The pomegranate symbolizes large families. You bought the container. It must have reminded you of your brothers and your sister at home."

"You should keep it for exactly the same reason! Is it not true that you are an only child?" Yingtai asked triumphantly.

"So?" Shanbo was not sure what she was trying to say.

"So you should keep it. You will have a lot of children when you get married."

"I want the same thing for you too," Shanbo said.

"Whatever you have, I will have, some day," Yingtai said, thinking that he would perhaps finally understand.

"I don't understand." Shanbo replied.

Yingtai looked at him helplessly. "Shanbo, this is all I can tell you at the moment. Someday you will understand."

"Sometimes you make absolutely no sense to me, Yingtai!"

Yingtai thought it incredible that Shanbo could not think along the right lines. "Sometimes Shanbo, you should do more than just read books!" she said.

Shanbo was going to say something but she stopped him. "Take this paperweight, please. I would prefer that you keep it. I have many more at home."

"But you like it very much. You always use it when you read."

"Yes, that is why I want you to keep it. It has very special meaning for me. Do you see these two butterflies inside? I hope that we will always be as close to each other as they are."

"Are you sure you want to give this to me? I think you love this paperweight more than anything else."

"Yes, I am sure. It takes on a new meaning now. When you look at the butterflies, you will see them as representing you and me. And in time you will understand everything."

"Wait, wait. These butterflies are a couple. See, this one is male, this female. They cannot be you and me."

"They can if you want them to." Yingtai almost wanted to scream into his face and tell him how stupid he was. She had already opened the door for him. All he needed to do was go into the room and find out what was there. But he would not go through that door. Yingtai was feeling so desperate that she began to laugh uncontrollably.

Shanbo looked at her in dismay. "What is so funny?"

"You are really dense sometimes, Shanbo. I don't know what to say to you any more. No more questions. Keep these, just because I want you to have them, all right?" She put the mandarin ducks, the pen container, and the paperweight onto Shanbo's desk.

Shanbo apparently found it hard to take Yingtai's words. "What else do you have to tell me?"

Yingtai thought to herself: what else do I have to tell him? He is so hopeless! "I have said enough. Now you need to do some creative thinking. When we leave tomorrow, maybe I will tell you more."

Shanbo was very disturbed for the rest of the day. It was hard to believe that Yingtai was leaving with so little notice. And he had spoken so cryptically! Shanbo was more puzzled than ever about Yingtai. Then he told himself that Yingtai was probably very sad and could not think straight and ended up saying strange things.

After dinner Shun Wang came to take most of the luggage and set off, leaving the lightest bags for Yinxin.

Yingtai and Shanbo sat together in Shanbo's room for the last evening. Neither knew what to say. They sat trying to look at each other yet avoid meeting each other's eyes. Shanbo broke the silence.

"I don't think I am going to stay here for long without you. I might leave for home soon after you. Anyway, I have already learned quite a lot over the past three years."

Yingtai brightened up a little. "And you will come and see me soon?"

"Yes, as soon as I can." Shanbo assured her.

"You know, after I get home, all that matters to me is the hope of seeing you again."

"I think you may have some good news for me by the time we meet again," Shanbo said.

The words "good news" made Yingtai's heart go faster. "What good thing could happen to me?"

"I have been thinking of this. If your mother is not really ill and you have been called back with such urgency, it may well be that your parents have found you a bride. If so, I will be very happy for you."

"How could you even think of something like that, you little bookworm?" she blurted.

At first hearing the word "bride," Yingtai was so happy that she almost said that he could have her as his bride if he asked her father for permission. She had to make a special effort to press down the impulse. But when she heard the rest of his statement, she said, "You are making wild guesses. Just wait and see. Everything will be clear to you very soon."

"Is that so?" Shanbo could not bring himself to take Yingtai's words too seriously. He had gotten used to Yingtai's cryptic conversations and mysterious behavior. Instead of suspecting anything, he found it all rather amusing and endearing.

With that, they started joking with each other. This helped them to forget the pain of the impending separation. They talked and laughed until Sijiu came to warn them about the time.

CHAPTER 9

EARLY NEXT MORNING Yinxin and Sijiu came to wake their masters up. After breakfast they started walking downhill.

It was a sunny day. Sijiu was carrying the luggage while Yinxin was walking next to him with the horse. Yingtai and Shanbo followed at a distance. The bamboo had grown much taller, stronger and denser than it had been three years before. Yingtai stretched out her arms to touch the leaves as she walked.

"They say that Master Zhou's school is enjoying a better reputation over time. Look, even the bamboo grows well here. They say that this means there are good students here too. Which of us do you think will be successful in the future?" Yingtai asked Shanbo.

"If you ask me, I would say you will be the most successful."

"Come on, you are only saying this because we are brothers."

"But I have my reasons. Our classmates have said there is something about you that is feminine and I agree. If you look at the most famous people in history, they all shared this feminine quality in one way or another. When the time comes for making major decisions, it is usually this kind of person who is able to make quick and great moves. These people generally prove to be much stronger in spirit than those who only look strong in appearance. I think you are one of those people."

"You are flattering me! How can I be compared with historical heroes? Well, let us talk about something much closer to reality."

"Like what?"

"Like how you will send my best wishes on to your parents when you get home," Yingtai said.

"Sure. And please do the same thing for me when you are back with your parents."

"I will." Yingtai said. "I believe your parents will be thinking of finding you a bride soon."

"Who do you think will want to marry a poor student like me? Your family is rich. I am sure there will be plenty of girls wanting to marry you. Like I said yesterday, I suspect they have already found someone for you," Shanbo suggested. "When you do get married, please don't forget your poor sworn-brother."

"You don't know what you are talking about." Yingtai became irritated and disturbed. "I am never going to marry anyone. I will stay close to you for the rest of my life." Her face turned very red with repressed passion.

Shanbo was shocked to see Yingtai responding to his joke so strongly. He never dared to imagine the prospect of Yingtai spending the rest of his life with him. But he did not want to upset him further and said, "I only wish that could be possible."

"It will be, trust me." Once again, Yingtai was hoping to arouse Shanbo's suspicion but not enough to reveal the truth, since she knew Mrs. Zhou would do it for her soon after she was gone. She decided not to go any further.

By now, they had entered the city of Hangzhou. It was still early. A few peasants were going into town to sell firewood. Yingtai was perplexed. "They are such hard working people. They must have been in the mountain chopping wood in the middle of the night in order to sell it early in the morning."

"These people live in the small towns nearby. They got the firewood ready a few days ago, and then left for market early in the morning like we did. After they have sold the wood in the morning, they go shopping in the afternoon so that they can bring provisions home in the evening."

Yingtai blinked, and said, "So they work hard and get up extremely early all for the benefit of their families, eh? Well Shanbo, I think you are doing something quite similar."

"No, how can what I am doing be similar? They do it for their wives and children at home, but I do this for my brother. It is very different," Shanbo said, a little bewildered.

Yingtai found herself wordless again. "How dense you are! Try to use your imagination for once!" was all she could say to him.

Shanbo did not respond to that. He sensed that there was a message that Yingtai was desperate to convey to him. But Yingtai seemed determined not to state it explicitly. He decided to be patient and wait.

They passed through the city quickly. On the way to a neighboring town, Yingtai saw a pavilion not very far ahead and suggested they stop and take a rest.

"It has been three years since we first met at one of these pavilions. I cannot believe that time has passed so rapidly!" Yingtai commented as they walked up to the pavilion.

Shanbo looked around and reminded Yingtai of the two visits they had paid to a garden close by. "I love the peonies there. They are probably the best peonies in this part of the country. Too bad we cannot take any with us."

Yingtai saw her chance again. "You have yet to see the peonies in my garden. If you come to visit me shortly, all the peonies there can be yours. But you must not wait too long, or else they will all be past bloom."

Shanbo looked confused.

"Ha ha, I know you still don't understand. Take your time and think a bit more. I will continue to say strange things, just so you will have plenty to occupy your mind when I am gone," Yingtai said playfully.

They moved on. Yingtai was busy finding things to say that could lead Shanbo onto the right track. After a while, a stream was in sight. The current was swift until it got to a lower spot where a pond was formed. Some white geese were swimming in it. Yingtai drew Shanbo's attention to them.

"Mm, this is a nice sight," Shanbo remarked. As they walked nearer to the stream, they could hear the sound of water sweeping the sand in the bed of the stream.

"Stream, sand, pond, geese, and grass along the bank ... I could spend a whole day here," Shanbo murmured.

"Do you hear the geese saying something?" Yingtai asked.

"What?" Shanbo was alert. He could sense that Yingtai was going to say odd things again.

"Can you detect something romantic there? Those swimming ahead are male geese; those following are female ones. The females are making the sound to make sure that they don't lose the males. What they are saying is 'brother, brother'."

Yinxin, on hearing what Yingtai said, playfully said to Sijiu, "Master Liang is walking in the front. He looks just like a male goose!"

Shanbo was amused. "Don't be so silly, Yingtai. How can you tell that the geese are calling 'brother?' Yinxin, your statement is ridiculous. How can you compare me to a male goose?"

Yingtai was frustrated: this man simply refused to come out of the brotherhood. "Time will tell who is the silly one, Shanbo," she said.

The stream became wider as they followed its path, the current getting swifter. They reached the point where they had to cross the stream. A few large rocks were placed irregularly across the stream for people to walk across upon. Having never experienced crossing like this before, Yingtai burst out, "I cannot do this! I am too scared!"

Shanbo tried to calm her. "No need to fear. I will figure something out."

"Look! There is a bridge over there," Sijiu cheered.

The bridge was narrow and made of wood. There were no rails to hang on to. Yingtai hesitated. Shanbo stretched out his hand. "Take my hand. I will lead the way."

The bridge proved to be very unsteady, swinging from one side to another. Yingtai was genuinely terrified. She pressed herself against Shanbo's back.

Shanbo assuringly put his hands on her arms that held his waist tightly.

They moved very slowly, one small step at a time.

When they got to the end of the bridge, Yingtai did not let go of Shanbo. Pressing her face against his shoulder, she said gratefully, "My entire life has been dependent upon you."

This was exactly how she felt. With Shanbo, she felt safe and secure.

Shanbo patted her hands and reminded her, "I can be with you only today. You have got to be a little stronger for the rest of the trip." He stretched his arms backward to push her around so that he could look her in the eyes.

Yingtai raised her head to meet his eyes. "I need your protection. Can you protect me for the rest of my life?" Her eyes were burning with hope and eagerness.

"I would love to, but there is no need. You are a strong person. You are more than capable of protecting yourself. Besides, you will have to be the protector yourself some day," Shanbo said, and gave her hands a hard grip.

"A protector for whom?"

"For ... well, for your wife and for your children."

Yingtai startled, realizing that she had totally forgotten the male role she had been playing. She let go of Shanbo, trying to hide her embarrassment by adjusting her clothes. In the midst of her confusion, something dropped to the ground. Shanbo picked it up.

"Wow, it is a pretty little jade butterfly," he exclaimed.

"Oh, this is for you. I was going to give it to you before we parted ways." Yingtai was glad that this had diverted Shanbo's attention from her abashment.

"I cannot accept this. You have given me too many gifts already. Besides, I can tell that this is a very expensive little jade butterfly."

"I want you to keep it. It is part of a couple, and I have the other one. When you finally come to see me, you will be holding both in your hands before you knock at my door."

"How can this be possible?"

"Well, this is another riddle for you to solve! Just keep this butterfly," Yingtai said.

"Oh well, it looks I have a lot of thinking to do after I get back to school."

"Exactly! So please make good use of your intelligence."

They had to walk through a small forest of pine trees before they could hit the main road. The pine trees grew very close to one another. No one else was in sight. They picked a path and followed it into the depth of the forest.

"Look, there is a graveyard right in front of us," Yinxin pointed out.

They went up to have a better look. A tombstone read: Joint Grave of Mr. and Mrs. Huishan Zhang.

"So this is where the husband and wife rest forever. They must have asked their children to make the common grave. What a good idea! They will be together forever like this," Yingtai said thoughtfully. "Shanbo, we can do the same thing when we die, so that we will never be apart. What do you think?"

"But we are men and we bear different last names. This could not work."

"If we want to make it work, it will work." Yingtai instantly became very disturbed, starting to show her willfulness again.

"All right, calm yourself. We will make it work somehow." Shanbo now knew how to deal with her when she was upset. "But we are still young. We have plenty of time to talk about this yet."

When they reached the main road, Yinxin and Sijiu were already far ahead of them. It took them a while to catch up with them. Yingtai was a little out of breath. They decided to take a rest.

They walked off the road to a small clearing and sat down under the shade of a huge tree.

"I wonder if we can find some water," Shanbo said as he looked around.

Just then, a peasant came toward them carrying a bucket of water. He told them that there was a well close by.

Upon hearing this, Yinxin and Sijiu livened up and ran to the well. The well was about the size of a table, with water up to the brim. The water was so calm and clear that it could almost serve as a mirror. A dried squash was cut into two halves, making two ladles for people to drink from.

"This is great. We can drink to our hearts' content!" Sijiu cried.

Shanbo tasted the water, and handed the ladle to Yingtai. "This must be water from a spring. It is very sweet."

Yingtai drank slowly until Yinxin and Sijiu finished drinking and ran away.

"The water is very clear. I want to check whether we can see ourselves in the well. Do you want to do that with me?"

They looked down onto the well together. There they were. Shanbo was handsome and well-built. Yingtai was handsome in a rather cute way. Tenderness was shown in her eyes.

Yingtai leaned against Shanbo's shoulder and said, "We make a perfect couple." Stirring the water with her hand, she was happy to see the two of them blending into each other.

"But we both are men. Two men don't make a couple," Shanbo corrected her.

"We could if one of us were really a woman." The words slipped out before Yingtai could stop herself. She was as shocked as Shanbo who stared at her tongue-tied.

"Does that make sense to you if one of us were a woman?" She tried to say it in a casual manner this time.

"Yes, but you are talking about impossibilities," Shanbo found his voice back at this. "Neither of us is a woman!"

"Then don't take it so seriously. It is just something frivolous to talk about on the road." By this time, Yingtai was pretty much convinced that Shanbo would never come to the truth on his own. She congratulated herself on having had the foresight and courage to speak with Mrs. Zhou. Otherwise, she could not imagine how much difficulty she would have trying to explain it all to Shanbo on her own.

They walked on and eventually came to a temple. "This is where people come for their wedding. They want the blessing of the Guanyin Buddha who is supposed to bring people children." While Yingtai said this, an idea came to her mind.

"Speaking about weddings, I want to be sure of something. Are you positive that your parents have not yet found you a bride?"

"Yes, I am positive. No, they have not found me a bride. Why?" Shanbo was again bewildered.

"It just occurred to me that my sister would make the perfect bride for you. Remember I told you the day we met that I had a sister who was educated at home and who could not come with me to Hangzhou?"

"Yes."

"If you two marry, you and I could actually always be together," Yingtai said.

"But what would your parents think of the idea? I don't have much to offer her in terms of wealth. And you know how important family backgrounds are when it comes to marriage." Shanbo did not want to get excited for nothing.

"I will talk with my parents as soon as I get home. I know it will be more important for them that you are a well-educated man, and I know how good a person you are. I can put in a lot of good words for you."

"How old is your sister?" Shanbo was getting interested.

"She is ... exactly my age. I mean she is my twin sister." Yingtai was amazed that she could make up such a story so quickly.

"Your twin sister? How come you never mentioned this before? Does she look like you?"

"She looks exactly like me."

"You are not making all this all up, are you?" Shanbo was beginning to think that this was too good to be true.

"Why would I make this up? You knew I had a sister!" Yingtai said defensively, a smile escaping from her lips.

"Then why are you smiling?"

"I am smiling because you are being so silly." Yingtai lost control of herself and burst into laughter. She laughed until tears came out. Then she began to cry.

"Yingtai, are you all right?" Shanbo asked anxiously.

"Yes, but it is getting late. I think you should turn back," Yingtai wept.

Shanbo was saddened as he looked at the sun. He knew he should start walking back. He had walked with Yingtai for about seven miles already.

"Sooner or later, we have to say good-bye. Let us part now." Very depressed, Shanbo took Yingtai's hands into his.

"Take good care of yourself and have a safe trip. I will come to see you and make the proposal to your father very soon."

"Please come in no more than a month's time. I will be waiting for you every day."

"I promise. I will come to see you." Shanbo could hardly fight back his tears.

Yinxin helped Yingtai onto the horse. Sijiu handed the luggage to her. They, too, were very sad when they said good-bye to each other. Then Sijiu bowed to Yingtai, and Yinxin bowed to Shanbo.

Shanbo and Sijiu stood motionless watching Yingtai and Yinxin slowly walking further and further away. Yingtai turned back to see Shanbo getting smaller in the distance, tears running down her cheeks each time she blinked.

CHAPTER 10

BACK AT SCHOOL, Shanbo could scarcely focus on his study. Sitting in the room only reinforced the emptiness he felt without Yingtai. All of a sudden, everything lost meaning, and he did not know what to do with himself any more. The life familiar to him disappeared with Yingtai.

Shanbo retired to bed early. Tired as he was, his mind was extremely active. He thought of Yingtai and his riddles. He felt strongly that there was something important he did not know about Yingtai. What could it be? He tried to imagine Yingtai's twin sister. He kept trying to put Yingtai into woman's clothing in his mind but could not visualize her well. He was glad that Yingtai mentioned the marriage possibility. That would be the best connection he could have with Yingtai.

The next morning, Shanbo went about his routine absent-mindedly. Lunch was tasteless, and he gave up reading. He lay in bed in desperation, trying to decide what he should do with himself.

A messenger came and told him that Mrs. Zhou wanted to see him. Shanbo was taken by surprise. Why did she want to see him? They had never exchanged anything more than polite greetings.

Mrs. Zhou was already waiting for him in the sitting room. She asked him to sit down and said, "I need to speak with you about something."

Shanbo looked at her expectantly.

"Master Zhou has always said that you are a wonderful student. I have no doubt about that. But perhaps you put too much into your study, and ignored some details of everyday life. No wonder some of your classmates called you a bookworm."

Shanbo smiled helplessly, not having a clue of what she was trying to say.

"Let me get straight to the point. You have been living and studying with Yingtai for three years. Do you think it was a man or a woman you were doing all of this with?"

Shanbo was astounded. "Is Yingtai a woman? It never crossed my mind that he could be a woman!"

"Yingtai was and is a woman. She wanted me to reveal this to you." Mrs. Zhou looked at Shanbo pitifully, seeing him struggle with disbelief and amazement.

"My! My! Yingtai was a woman! He was a woman! A woman he—she is!" Shanbo looked as if he had been given a heavy blow. All of a sudden, everything strange about Yingtai had an explanation. "Of course she is a woman!" He was overwhelmed with astonishment. He talked to himself aloud to make things more credible.

Mrs. Zhou looked at him with sympathy and amusement.

"But he told me that he had a twin sister, and even suggested that I should propose to their father."

"That is because she could not just offer herself to you. Now do you understand, Mr. Bookworm?" Mrs. Zhou questioned.

"So Yingtai is her own sister?" Shanbo still could not believe his ears.

"Yes, and this is what Yingtai wanted me to give you." Mrs. Zhou took out the jade butterfly and extended it to Shanbo. "She wanted me to tell you that you are the only man she would marry."

Shanbo was dumbfounded. The jade butterfly was exactly the same as the one Yingtai had given him the day before!

"Oh, I am the biggest fool in the world!" he cried out aloud, losing his usual reserve completely. All the riddles and strange things Yingtai had done came back to him and began to make perfect sense.

"Now, what are you going to do, lucky man?" Mrs. Zhou woke him up from the shock, confusion, and rising happiness.

"Oh, yes. I must do something about it. And I must not lose any time. Does Master Zhou know about this?"

"He is the second biggest fool in the world. He knew only when I told him so."

"What does he think?" Shanbo wanted to make sure that Master would understand what he was about to do.

"Actually, he is the one who urged me to tell you the truth. He thinks that you should go as soon as you can to propose to Yingtai's parents. You don't find a bride like Yingtai every day, you know."

Shanbo was delighted to hear that. "Thank you both so much. I will have to make a quick decision as to when I leave. With the way things are at the moment, I think I would like to leave in two days. I will notify you as soon as I am ready." He bowed to Mrs. Zhou again to thank her.

Before turning to the door, he stopped short and asked, "So I guess Yinxin is a woman too."

"What do you think?" Mrs. Zhou laughed.

"Wow, what news! Sijiu will be shocked and happy too!"

Shanbo flew out of the house back to his room, beside himself with mixed feelings: he was definitely shocked, he was surely excited, and above all, he was extremely happy.

The first thing he did when he got back to his room was to put the two jade butterflies together. He remembered that Yingtai wanted him to take both of them along when he went to see her father. He found a piece of cloth and wrapped them up carefully.

Then he put the butterfly paperweight, the bronze mandarin ducks, and the pomegranate pen container together. Recalling what Yingtai said when she gave them to him, he could not help berating himself for being so stupid.

"Yingtai had tried so hard to give me hints. How could I have been so blind?" Shanbo shook his head as he put them away.

"How could I have swallowed that weak explanation about her pierced ears?" Shanbo was talking aloud to himself again. "How could I involve myself with the silly game of putting the bowls of water between us before I could sleep next to her? Whose mother would play such a stupid game with her son? But Yingtai found a fool to do it with her!" Shanbo slapped himself on the head as he replayed the scene in his mind. "But then again, she was just being a good woman. She could not sleep with a man, but she, as my brother, could not reject me either. No wonder she never did anything private with me or in my presence. She would not let me go to the bathroom with her even when she could barely walk! Oh, what a hard time I gave her!" Shanbo stamped his foot on the floor, totally disgusted with himself.

"What is this, Master Liang?" Shanbo was so tense with his thoughts that he did not notice Sijiu had walked into the room.

"Here you are! Are you sure you want to know this?" Shanbo was thrilled that he would find an outlet talking with Sijiu.

Sijiu was mystified. He had never seen his Master so excited and so out of control. "Please tell me what has happened." His curiosity very much aroused.

"Now prepare yourself for the shock of your life. You probably will not get over it ever."

Sijiu's eyes opened wide.

"Do you know the important difference between Yingtai and me, and between Yinxin and you?" Pleased to see that Sijiu was confused by his question, Shanbo breathed out one word after another, "They are both women."

Sijiu's mouth opened wide, his eyes wider than before. "They are both women?" he repeated mechanically.

"You heard it correctly," Shanbo confirmed, sympathetic with Sijiu. He had not got over the shock himself.

"So what do we do about it?" Sijiu did not even know how to think any more.

"We can do a lot about it. I want to leave here as soon as possible. More importantly, I want to marry Yingtai."

"Great! Then I can marry Yinxin and we will take care of you together." Sijiu was quick to respond.

"Smart thought! Why have you not used your smartness earlier?" Shanbo joked.

"Why would I have even thought of it? They were crazy to do that!" Sijiu complained.

"True, it really was a crazy thing to do. So crazy that we men did not even come close to suspecting anything, though with hindsight, I can easily find flaws in what they did and said." Shanbo was suddenly filled with admiration for Yingtai for taking on such a challenge in a man's world.

"We should get ready to go. I will start packing tomorrow." Sijiu wanted action.

A sleepless night followed. Shanbo indulged himself in reliving the time he had spent with Yingtai. His heart pounded violently as he kept asking himself how it could be possible that he shared a bed with Yingtai for five nights without knowing she was a woman? He tried to recollect how it felt sleeping so near to her and wished he could go back in time. But if he had known then what he knew now, would he have dared to hold her like he did? Would she have let him do it?

He remembered all the things Yingtai had said when he walked her part way back that morning. She must have been very disappointed by his dumbness. She had so lovingly talked about letting him have all the peonies in her garden. She had clung so fast to him for protection when crossing the bridge. She had been so openly upset when he talked about her marrying someone. She had so affectionately given him the jade butterfly. She had so determinedly said that she would share a grave with him after they died. She had so passionately looked at their reflection in the well with him, pressing her head against him. She had gone so far as to invent a sister for him to marry, only to show him how much she felt for him! But what did he say to her? He accused her of being childish and ridiculous, of not making any sense. He deserved to be called a bookworm. She must have thought that he was a cold-hearted creature!

He began to feel an acute pain, the pain of letting Yingtai down, the pain of missing her, the pain of failing to enjoy the best moments with her, the pain of not being able to show her how much he cared for her, not as brother to brother, but as man to woman, and the pain of owing her so much love.

He tried to remember how it felt when Yingtai was so intimate with him. His hands seemed to be able to feel the warmth of her hands. His back seemed to be able to feel her weight as he recalled how she crossed the bridge after him. He remembered her smell when she leaned against him by the well. Oh, what an idiot he was in letting those precious moments go by!

He slept a little at dawn. He found himself wandering in a garden of peonies. One peony was especially large and in perfect bloom. There was something unusual about it that made him stop. He looked into the center of the flower. It began to change shape and suddenly it turned into Yingtai's face. She walked out of the peony toward him in a flowery shirt and skirt, her eyes filled with tears of happiness, and her arms stretching out for him. He had never seen her in woman's clothes and she was more beautiful than any of the flowers around. For a moment, Shanbo was intoxicated, gazing into her face with admiration. Suddenly, Yingtai became vague, and vanished into the air ...

"Yingtai!" Shanbo cried out and went wild with an acute sense of loss. He jumped up and down violently in complete dismay, not knowing where to look for her.

He was woken up by the noise he made and found himself sitting in bed, exhausted by the intense emotions he had experienced in the dream. He was drenched in sweat.

For the next couple of days, Shanbo and Sijiu were busy packing and saying good-bye to friends. Shanbo paid the last visit to Master Zhou who was in full support of his decision, and thanked him for his teaching of three years.

Shanbo's horse died of old age the second year he was at the school, so they had to walk home. Shanbo was not at all discouraged because he could see Yingtai waiting for him at the end of the journey.

CHAPTER 11

BACK IN THE Zhu Village, Yingtai's parents were getting ready for their daughter's return. They had good news for Yingtai. Mrs. Zhu was by no means sick. She was in good shape. She missed Yingtai, and was hoping she could spend some time with her before marrying her off. They knew that Yingtai might not come back for an arranged marriage, so they gave her a reason she could not refuse.

It had all happened a month before. Gongyuan Zhu went to a gathering in town where he met the rich and powerful Taishou Ma, who had control over the army of the region. While drinking, they talked about their children. Gongyuan Zhu learned that Taishou Ma had three sons, the two older ones already married, with the youngest one still attending school. Taishou Ma, who had long heard of the beauty and talent of Gongyuan Zhu's only daughter, approached him with special interest. The two men got along very well, drinking and eating merrily until both were quite drunk.

A few days later, Taishou Ma sent for Gongyuan Zhu, inviting him to a family dinner. Gongyuan Zhu, thinking that Taishou Ma must think highly of him, was extremely flattered to be treated by this most powerful man in the area. At dinner, he came to know Wencai Ma, a handsome young man who was introduced as the youngest and most promising son of the

Ma family. Wencai Ma sat next to him, making sure that he was properly served. Gongyuan Zhu decided that he was smart, though boastful and frivolous at times, but that was how children from rich families often were.

About ten days later, Matchmaker Qiu came to the door of the Zhu family. The best-known go-between in the area, Qiu possessed the glibbest tongue in her trade. She was determined to do this job well for she knew there was big money involved.

As soon as Gongyuan Zhu and Mrs. Zhu came to the sitting room, Matchmaker Qiu greeted them with a big grin and a deep bow. "Congratulations!" she said exaggeratedly. "I am honored to be called upon by Taishou Ma to come here to inquire about the possibility of a marriage between his youngest son and your darling daughter," she started in a straightforward manner.

Gongyuan Zhu and Mrs. Zhu were not prepared for this surprise. They looked at each other, unable to react right away. It then dawned on Gongyuan Zhu why Taishou Ma had given him so much attention.

"Thank you for coming. We are most honored that Taishou Ma thinks that our daughter is worthy of his son," said Gongyuan Zhu. He cleared his throat to hide his thoughts. He then decided that he should show Matchmaker Qiu some authority as host.

"Now relax and have some tea. We would love to hear more about the family and, of course, the beloved son of the family."

Matchmaker Qiu adjusted her position a little and continued, "Wencai Ma is twenty four years old. He is handsome, charming, and well-educated. He is dutiful to his parents, respectful to his brothers and sisters-in-law, and kind to his servants. He neither drinks nor smokes. He is a perfect young man, if you ask me. Such a man deserves an excellent wife. Wencai Ma will not satisfy himself with an average woman. He has rejected at least a dozen girls, either because they were not beautiful enough, or not intelligent enough. But when he heard of Miss Yingtai Zhu, he was very impressed and wanted me to pay you a visit immediately."

She paused to get back her breath. "As far as I can see, these two young people are destined to live their lives together. And the two families are well-matched in social and economic status too. To be honest, I have been a go-between all my life, and never saw a better match than this one!" she said, observing Gongyuan Zhu and Mrs. Zhu's response. "What will you say to this perfect match, Mr. and Mrs. Zhu?"

To such a too-good-to-be-true description, Gongyuan Zhu was tempted to give a positive response. He tried to flash back a picture of the young man in his mind. Obviously, he was not as perfect as Matchmaker Qiu proclaimed, but he would definitely be good enough for his Yingtai. Besides, the Mas were the most prominent and wealthy family in the region. If Yingtai married Wencai Ma, she would enjoy a far more comfortable life than he himself could ever provide her. What else could a father hope for his daughter in marriage anyway?

Gongyuan Zhu turned to his wife. "I met Wencai Ma when I was invited to dinner by his father. He was indeed handsome and quite intelligent. I believe he would be good for our daughter. Since Taishou Ma had asked Matchmaker Qiu to convey his good will, perhaps we should give her a definite answer?"

Mrs. Zhu hesitated, then said, "Marriage is a matter of a lifetime. I think we had better give it more thought."

Matchmaker Qiu was covertly happy when Gongyuan Zhu spoke so favorably to Mrs. Zhu, but was a bit dejected that the latter was not so ready to give her consent. Gathering herself together, she revealed her thoughts.

"Mrs. Zhu, let me tell you something. I can say for sure that you will never regret doing this for your daughter. Frankly, such a match cannot be found in a hundred years. I am in the best position to assure you that the Ma family is the best you will find around here. What is better, Wencai Ma is such a talented and promising young man. It is hard to find a young man like him these days. I cannot tell you how many parents desire him to be their son-in-law. You are most fortunate in that both he and his father are interested in your daughter. It is as if someone had placed delicious meat into your mouth. How can you afford to spit it out?"

Seeing that Mrs. Zhu was not very much impressed, she changed the tone of her voice, and warned, "I am not saying this to threaten you, but Taishou Ma can be very nasty if he is offended. You should choose to be friends with him rather than become his enemy."

These words had an effect upon Gongyuan Zhu. Why would he want to make himself an enemy to Taishou Ma? His retirement had lowered him to the status of an ordinary person. It would be his and Yingtai's good fortune to be able to forge such a connection with the powerful Ma family. This would guarantee happiness for the rest of Yingtai's life too. He did not see why he should resist such an offer. He was about to give his consent when he saw his wife making disturbed eye contact with him. Failing to make out anything from that, he found an excuse to leave the room. Mrs. Zhu came right after him.

"What do you think?" Gongyuan Zhu asked.

Mrs. Zhu looked worried. "I don't think we should give consent so soon. We need to find out whether Matchmaker Qiu is telling us the truth. On the other hand, I think Yingtai needs to be consulted on the matter. You know her well enough. Otherwise, there may be consequences."

Gongyuan Zhu pondered for a while, and agreed.

"You are right to some extent. However, parents are supposed to arrange marriages for their children. Yingtai has always had her way with us. She simply has to obey us this one time. We do this for her own benefit anyway. If we confirm that Wencai Ma is a promising young man, we should agree to the marriage. Besides, if Yingtai married into such a powerful family, it would be her good luck and our honor."

Mrs. Zhu concluded that that was the best they could do for the time being. "We will tell Matchmaker Qiu that we need some time to think it over, and that she should come to hear our decision at a later time."

Matchmaker Qiu was a little disappointed to be told to wait. But since the Zhus did not show an outright negative attitude, she decided that it was the best she could do for the moment. Before leaving, she urged the Zhus to be quick with their decision.

As a result of this meeting, Yingtai was called home. She was nineteen years old, and Gongyuan Zhu thought it almost too old an age to get married. He planned to get Yingtai ready for the wedding as soon as he was convinced that Wencai Ma had all the good qualities Matchmaker Qiu claimed that he had.

CHAPTER 12

YINGTAI AND YINXIN were on the road for five days. They had talked about nothing but the prospect of seeing Shanbo again. Yinxin was delighted to know that Shanbo would know their secret soon. She teased Yingtai all the way, and Yingtai joked about Sijiu and her. The two were so happy fantasizing about their future that the trip was over before they had realized it.

It was almost noon time when they approached the Zhu Village. "I believe Shun Wang made it back yesterday. They must be expecting us by the gate now," Yingtai said, looking hard into the distance.

"I can still remember the day when we left. I cannot believe we are back already," said Yinxin.

"It feels like only yesterday that I had such trouble trying to convince my father to let me go. Looking back, I can sympathize with him. Who knew what could have happened with his daughter so far out of his reach? I could have stayed away forever! If it were not for this radical change in appearance, I could have never made this trip. I would venture a guess that in a thousand years, it will be common for women to leave home and educate themselves at school just like men have always done."

"Even so, you were lucky enough to get your parents' permission to do it now. You succeeded in getting yourself an education. Plus, you also found yourself a man!"

"Not so loud Yinxin! You have got to keep quiet about it for the next day or so. I need to find a good way to introduce the subject to my parents," Yingtai warned Yinxin.

"You can count on me for secrecy and support," Yinxin assured her.

As they were talking, they moved closer to home. As expected, a crowd was waiting for them by the gate. The servants all came up to help. Instantly, Yingtai was off the horse and the luggage that Yinxin carried was taken away.

"Have I changed a lot?" Yingtai asked joyfully. Her mind was so preoccupied by the thought of Shanbo that she did not really think about home until this very moment. At seeing all the familiar faces and things, she began to realize that she had been a little homesick after all.

"You look exactly the same," they replied.

"You are all fibbing. How can I be the same dressed in man's clothing?" Yingtai said, laughing. "But you are correct, I am indeed the same person."

She went into the house, and made for the sitting room where her parents were waiting for her with all smiles. She went forward and bowed to them.

"You don't have to bow to us," her mother said blissfully.

"It is all right. She is still in her male student clothes," Gongyuan Zhu said delightfully.

"How are you, mother? You look well to me," Yingtai inquired.

"I am fine, my daughter. I was not feeling very well last ten days or so. Your father must have exaggerated it in the letter. We asked you to return because we both missed you so much," Mrs. Zhu answered.

Yingtai and Yinxin exchanged a look.

"It has been a long journey for you. Now go and freshen up. We will have plenty of time to talk," said her father.

When Yingtai changed back into her own clothes, she took a good look at herself in the bronze mirror. She could barely remember how she had looked dressed as a girl. In fact, she had developed fully into a young woman while she was away at school. She looked delightfully fresh and charming in the reflection. The jewels in her hair highlighted her charms, and the full length belted dress accentuated her gracefulness.

Yingtai tried to imagine how Shanbo would react when he saw her dressed as she was now. She fantasized that she could see Shanbo standing next to her in the reflection. He was all smiling. She was so intoxicated by his smile and by the tenderness that shone in his eyes that she imagined that she could feel herself leaning against his chest, and that Shanbo put his arms around her ...

Yingtai blushed at these intimate thoughts. Now that she was alone, she realized how much she missed Shanbo and how much she wanted to be with him.

At dinner that evening, her parents asked in great detail about her life at the school. Yingtai told them everything except her relationship with Shanbo. After dinner, she stayed with her parents for a while.

"Father, I promised you three things before I left home. Now that I have returned as soon as I heard that mother was ill, and since no one had any idea that I was really a girl at school, I have already satisfied two of these promises. I am now ready for the third, the medical check-up."

It took Gongyuan Zhu a while to understand what Yingtai was talking about. He was somewhat ashamed of what he had made Yingtai promise, but did not know how to avoid the embarrassment of checking to see whether Yingtai was still a virgin.

Mrs. Zhu came to her husband's rescue.

"This is not an urgent matter. Since Yingtai is so sure of herself, we will just take her word for it. I knew she would be a good girl." She turned to Yingtai and changed the topic by talking about the local specialties in Hangzhou.

When the business of resettling back into the household was over, Yingtai felt listless. Life at home became more oppressive than ever. She could either shut herself in her room reading or embroidering, or take walks in the garden. But that was all. No walks after dinner in the countryside, no classmates, no excursions anywhere, and above all, no Shanbo next to her. It was only after she had tasted freedom that she really knew what a secluded life she lived. However, she would not mind leading such an isolated life if only she could live it with Shanbo.

She tried to read, but words had no meaning to her. They would fade and Shanbo's face would appear on the page. Yingtai felt that Shanbo was blaming her for keeping her secret for three long years. He was upset that they had wasted time, and that he had never guessed the true meaning behind the games and tricks she played upon him. She wanted to explain everything to him, but each time she tried, his image would disappear from the page. Words would reappear on the page, but they still did not make any sense to her.

Then she would try embroidery, believing that she would enjoy picking up needlework again. But she kept pricking herself with the needle, too absent-minded to concentrate. She finally motivated herself to make something beautiful for Shanbo. She thought of a couple of butterflies. Yes, butterflies. She loved butterflies. They were so colorful and they lived in such a colorful world. She had seen them chasing each other among flowers. Imagine that! She envied them their freedom, even more for the fact that they could fly high and low. Their world was beyond control or restriction.

Inspired by this idea, Yingtai set to work. She made a sketch on a piece of white fabric: the butterfly that was to represent Shanbo would be the larger of the two and would have blue as its primary color. Blue was the color that Shanbo wore most of the time. The one that represented her would be smaller, and basically pink in color. She placed them flying together, with Shanbo a bit ahead of Yingtai, and their wings touching each other. As she completed the sketch, she could almost see herself flying with Shanbo.

When she needed a break from sewing, she would go out into the garden, the only place she was allowed outdoors. The peonies were in full bloom. She remembered telling Shanbo that he could have all of them. Mrs. Zhou should have told him the truth by now. Was he planning to come?

Would he come sooner than he had promised?

Time was passing unbearably slowly. Only two days had gone by since she returned home. How could three years have slipped away so fast when she was with Shanbo? Where was Shanbo now? How soon would he come? Tormented by the hollowness she felt without Shanbo, Yingtai decided she must have a talk with her mother about her relationship with Shanbo. Otherwise, her parents would be angry with her for not letting them know the story beforehand. She believed her mother might be sympathetic with her, but her father would be angry at her for choosing her own husband. He was a man who believed in parental authority, though he had been very tolerant with her in many ways. Yingtai thought it would be better to let her mother deal with her father.

As she was hanging around in the garden, Yingtai noticed that her father had some guests over for the day. Someone seemed to be looking out at her from the sitting room window. Since she was never interested in family business events, she just turned and went back to her butterfly work.

That evening, she asked Yinxin to invite her mother to her room. When she looked at her mother in the eyes, Yingtai lost the courage to tell her story all at once. She had read a lot of stories, but a story such as her own was unheard of. A go-between was always needed. How could she be her own matchmaker? Oh, yes, mother should be the first person to know. If she understood, her support would give Yingtai the courage to approach her father.

"Do you have something to tell me, my child?" Mrs. Zhu inquired.

"Yes, yes, something very unusual, but very important." Yingtai had calmed down by now. "It is about my future."

"Your future?" Mrs. Zhu asked curiously.

"To be more specific, about my future with a man."

"Your future with a man?" These words sounded like an explosion to Mrs. Zhu. She had to steady herself by leaning against the desk she was sitting at.

"What is that supposed to mean?"

Mrs. Zhu's reaction was not a good sign for Yingtai. But there was no turning back. She started to tell the story of how she met Shanbo, how they ended up as roommates, how they studied and lived together, how they became sworn brothers, and how Shanbo took care of her when she had the cold ...

She was a little hesitant at first, but as soon as she started talking about Shanbo, she became very eloquent. She related the story in such a way that Mrs. Zhu was moved, nodding here and there to acknowledge that she was listening attentively.

"From all the time I spent with him, I believe he is the only man for me. In fact, I have asked Mrs. Zhou to reveal to him who I really am and left the pair of jade butterflies for him as a token. I also invented a twin sister of mine whom I invited him to marry. By now he should know what I meant and should be here to propose for me within the month." Yingtai could not believe that she could narrate the story with so much ease.

Mrs. Zhu was speechless at the story. After a long silence, she commented mechanically, "He sounds like a nice man."

"He really is," Yinxin, who had been standing aside, could not help throwing in good words. "He was exceptionally kind to my mistress. They would make a perfect couple."

"Will you please talk to father about it? I am afraid of telling him because I am sure he will be upset. You know that when he says no, he will not change his mind even if he knows he is wrong," Yingtai pleaded to her mother.

Mrs. Zhu looked at Yingtai with pride and sadness. Her daughter was very intelligent, maybe too intelligent to be a woman in a man's world. She did not know what to say to her. It would be cruel to disillusion her with reality. She wanted her daughter to keep her dream for a little longer.

"I understand you very well. We both know your father well too. He is a man who believes he can make all the decisions for everyone in his home. To be fair, he is better than most men. At least he listens to us sometimes. But he might be very tough on the marriage issue. He thinks it is most important that he be the decision-maker."

"That is why I turn to you for help. You are the only one who is likely to change his mind, if his mind can be changed at all," Yingtai said with despair. "Mother, you are my only hope, and this is the most important matter of my life!"

"Say no more. I know exactly how important it is. I cannot promise you anything, but I will try my best. Bear this in mind: hope for the best, but prepare for the worst."

With that, Mrs. Zhu turned and left. She was afraid that Yingtai would detect the sadness in her eyes.

Mrs. Zhu was put in a terrible dilemma. She wanted happiness for her daughter. She could tell that Yingtai and Shanbo were very much in love. But what was love? There was hardly such a word in the Chinese vocabulary when it came to feelings between a couple. The norm was that a man and a woman would hardly know each other before marriage. They usually never met each other until the wedding cere-mony. Everything was arranged by the parents through a matchmaker. Yingtai's experience with Shanbo was unprece-dented. Mrs. Zhu could hardly imagine that her husband would give consent to it.

But that was not the worst of it. On that very same morning, Matchmaker Qiu paid them another visit with Mrs. Ma in tow. No doubt the Ma family was giving this marriage a lot of attention since Taishou Ma sent his wife to catch a glimpse of Yingtai even before they agreed to the marriage. Fortunately, Yingtai had come back in time from Hangzhou. Otherwise, they would not have been able to find a valid explanation as to why Yingtai was not at home.

Mrs. Ma saw Yingtai when the latter came into the garden that morning. She did not try to hide her satisfaction with

Yingtai and said that her son would like Yingtai. While Mrs. Ma was getting into her horse carriage, Matchmaker Qiu found the opportunity to whisper to Gongyuan Zhu that Taishou Ma could not wait any longer. She made it clear that Taishou Ma would not take a "no" for answer. If the Zhus dared to go against his will, they would surely suffer the consequences.

Matchmaker Qiu went on to sweet talk about the material and political prospects Wencai Ma possessed and of the abundant betrothal presents they were prepared to give.

"Anyone in their right mind would agree to such a lucrative marriage," she concluded. "I don't understand why you have to even think about such an offer," she shook head as she said, "unless you are deliberately looking for trouble."

Gongyuan Zhu began to speak, "You are right. There is no point wasting any more time. Tell Taishou Ma that ..."

"Don't you think we should consult Yingtai about this? After all, it is her marriage we are talking about." Mrs. Zhu could not help cutting him short.

"There is absolutely no earthly reason why we should," Gongyuan Zhu said impatiently. "Our parents did not consult with us when they arranged our marriage. Do you think we are not wise enough parents to make this decision for Yingtai?" He gave his wife a critical look.

"Perhaps we should ask for a few articles Wencai Ma has written, so that Yingtai could judge for herself whether ..."

"Well, well, she can do all that later. I will ask them to bring along a few articles he has written when they bring over the betrothal presents." Matchmaker Qiu stopped her rudely.

"Enough," Gongyuan Zhu said with authority to keep his wife from saying any more. "It is settled. You can tell Taishou

Ma that we are both honored and flattered to accept the proposal of marriage between his son and our daughter. I will let the Mas choose the day for the wedding."

Matchmaker Qiu was overjoyed. "Thank you, Master Zhu. I will run to tell Taishou Ma at once. I believe they will send you the wedding gifts in just a few days."

With those words, Yingtai's future was determined. Although Mrs. Zhu was unhappy with the way the decision was made, she did not openly contradict her husband. Her major concern at the moment was that Yingtai should have been consulted for this matter. Now with Shanbo Liang coming into scene, the whole thing would get a lot worse. She knew for sure that Yingtai would despise this arranged marriage—she had always wanted to play a part in deciding her future. Worse yet, she had defied tradition by finding on her own a man to love. That was too radical even for Mrs. Zhu. Wonderful as Shanbo was, tradition held that Yingtai had no right to determine her own marriage. Now that her father had made the decision, Yingtai had to marry Taishou Ma's youngest son whether she liked him or not.

Mrs. Zhu shivered as she anticipated the conflict between her husband and her daughter. She knew neither of them would give up. Sighing, she sank into deep distress.

CHAPTER 13

MRS. ZHU SHOOK her head as she was trying to think of some way to help Yingtai. Though there did not seem to be any real solution, she still wanted to do something about it.

She walked into Gongyuan Zhu's study where he was sipping tea and reading.

"I just came back from a talk with Yingtai," she initiated.

"Oh, didn't we agree that we would not tell her about Wencai Ma until after the presents arrive?" Gongyuan Zhu asked casually.

"Yes. I did not tell her anything about that," Mrs. Zhu said. She thought it a good time to confront him now that he was relaxed,

"We talked about something else. Actually, it's a friend that Yingtai came to know well at school," she said, trying to make him interested.

"What about him?" Gongyuan Zhu stopped his reading.

"He is a very nice man called Shanbo Liang. He and Yingtai got on very well and became sworn brothers."

"Sworn brothers? Then what? I assume he did not know that Yingtai was a woman." Gongyuan Zhu was alert, staring at his wife for more details.

"Oh, no, of course not. According to Yingtai, it never crossed his mind that she was a woman. That's why she found him so reliable and ... charming!" Mrs. Zhu had picked that word carefully and knew it would change the conversation.

"Charming?! Wait a minute! She is not supposed to find any man charming!" Gongyuan Zhu got up, and walked to Mrs. Zhu. "So what else do you have to tell me?" He was working himself up to anger.

It would be a bad time to tell him the truth when he was angry, Mrs. Zhu thought, but he had already sensed something, and would not let her drop the subject.

"Well, what can we expect? Brotherhood means trusting and helping one another. Since Yingtai is a girl, she would not be blind to Shanbo's good qualities." Mrs. Zhu tried to avoid using strong words to describe the relationship.

"Now that she is home, what does she expect to do with him? Will he come to visit? Or are you saying that she wants to visit him?" Gongyuan Zhu could think of worse possibilities, but he chose not to.

"Yingtai feels that she can only... I mean, this man appears to be a good choice for her future." Mrs. Zhu stopped short here, waiting for her husband's reaction.

"Don't tell me that she is talking about marrying this man!" Gongyuan Zhu said in disbelief and rage, bending toward his wife.

"I am afraid that she is," Mrs. Zhu said gingerly.

"How dare she!" Words thundered out of Gongyuan Zhu as if they had a life of their own, startling Mrs. Zhu to a jump.

"I refuse to believe what you are saying!" he roared. "Yingtai has no say in this matter! Tell me no more about this ... what was his name? Never mind! I could care less about him. You can go tell Yingtai this second that I have already picked a husband for her." Gongyuan Zhu's voice lowered a bit as he made this authoritative statement.

"It is not going to be that simple. Shanbo is arriving in a few days to make his proposal."

Mrs. Zhu went on to give a brief account of the episode Yingtai had had with Mrs. Zhou before leaving school.

"This girl's behavior is scandalous!" Gongyuan Zhu cried in shock. "Are you telling me that she offered herself to this man without consulting us first?"

He became extremely agitated. "This is totally outrageous! Utterly Scandalous! Absolutely disgraceful!"

To emphasize his wrath, Gongyuan Zhu waved his fists in the air each time he used a new phrase, stamping his feet at the same time.

"You must go right now and tell her that she must forget all about this man because she is already betrothed to another!"

"But you know Yingtai. She always expects to get her way. This is something that will affect the rest of her life. You surely can't expect her to accept this without protest." Mrs. Zhu spoke softly, yet not failing to make her point.

"Have we not spoiled her enough? This is the consequence of letting her have her own way. She went to school, and came back a new person. Now she is choosing a husband for herself. Have you ever heard of such a thing? It is about time we exerted some control over her. No, 'authority' is the word."

"But what if Shanbo comes to propose?"

"We will tell him it is simply out of the question. Yingtai is engaged to somebody else, someone who is richer and more powerful," Gongyuan Zhu said condescendingly. "If he is as good as she says, he should feel shameful because surely he cannot compete with Wencai Ma."

He paused, and then added, "He is not even going about it in the proper way. There has to be a matchmaker. No one comes alone to propose by himself."

"What about Yingtai? Surely you don't expect her to stand for this?"

"She will just have to learn to accept it," Gongyuan Zhu said uncompromisingly.

The next day, Gongyuan Zhu left after breakfast. Yingtai looked at her mother searchingly. Mrs. Zhu's heart felt like it was being stung by a wasp. She was not ready to shatter Yingtai's hope.

"Your father was busy last night. And he has gone for two days. I will talk to him when he comes back." Avoiding eye contact, she managed a lie.

"Fine. I guess there is no need to hurry. I don't think Shanbo will arrive within the next three days. I just need father to be prepared for the visit," Yingtai said innocently.

Poor child, Mrs. Zhu said to herself. How would she take it? She shook her head sadly as she saw Yingtai leaving for her study.

Yingtai had a peaceful mind after telling Mrs. Zhu her story. From experience, she knew her mother would always end up her ally. All she needed to do was reason with her father. He was a reasonable man after all. If he refused to be convinced, she would resort to trickery and protest. She knew he could not bear to see her in misery.

Believing this, she spent the next few days in relative calm, happily fantasizing about Shanbo. She was so grateful that

Shanbo had been and would continue to be in her life. She occupied herself with only two things: lying in bed to recall her past as well as imagine her future with Shanbo, and working on the butterfly tapestry.

Her favorite memory was of the evenings when she and Shanbo were reading by the same candlelight. Many a time her eyes had wandered away from her book to his face. He was unaware of her attention, so that she could go over him with her gaze unnoticed. She loved the fact that he was there whenever she wanted to look at him and that he was available all the time. Looking back, it all felt like a dream. She even wondered whether she could handle such happiness when they were together again.

She also thought of the times when they had been physically intimate. How stupid she was not to allow herself to experience that as a woman at the time. She would stiffen as soon as Shanbo was close to her, then put herself on guard, only to yearn for his touch after he released her. Now she missed the sensation of feeling Shanbo the man, and she tried to imagine how it would feel to touch him as a woman. A thrilling wave swept over her. This feeling had never happened to her before and she was frightened—the books she had read never described in detail what men and women physically experienced when they made love, and she wondered if it felt anything like this.

She was ashamed of herself at such thoughts and returned to the embroidery. The butterflies were now taking form. The most difficult part was getting the wings properly done. She had unraveled two versions already because the butterflies did not fly right. She wanted to express the fluttering of the wings to show the stirring happiness of the butterflies. She would try a third time. She knew she would succeed because she felt the happiness within her.

Yingtai spent two happy days alone, living in a world of cherished memory and inspiring future. She looked forward to each new day, which gave her hope and substantiated her dreams.

The next was a brilliantly sunny day. Yingtai knew her father had gotten back late the night before, and she wondered whether her mother had found a chance to tell him about Shanbo. Deliberately, she did not go to breakfast, thinking that would give her parents the time to talk about Shanbo and her.

Things were very quiet for most of the morning. However, some time before lunch, there were loud noises at the front gate, which soon developed into a lot of commotion. Nothing like this had ever happened in the past. Yingtai was curious. She sent Yinxin to go and have a look.

"Miss, Miss," Yinxin flew back a few minutes later, "Congratulations! Master Liang is here. He is here to deliver the betrothal presents!"

The needle pricked Yingtai's finger as she jumped up from the chair.

"What? Say that again!" she cried nervously.

"I think Master Liang is here for you. He came with a lot of gifts," Yinxin said, beside herself with joy.

"Did you see Shanbo?" Yingtai asked anxiously.

"No, there were a lot of people moving about. I did not see Sijiu either. Master Zhu looked very happy telling the porters where to put things."

"Did you hear anything?"

"Yes, they said the wedding is coming up soon. Can you believe that? Master Liang must have left for home right after Mrs. Zhou talked with him."

Yingtai tried to bring herself under control. "Tell me what you saw. What were the gifts?"

"There were plenty of things. About a dozen rolls of silk fabric, I think."

"Yes?"

"A set of books, some writing brushes, Chinese ink sticks and inkstone."

"He knows what I like," Yingtai smiled.

"There is a lot of jewelry, too," Yinxin continued.

"A lot of jewelry? Are you sure?" Yingtai's heart began to sink.

"Yes, it must be worth a lot. It was dazzlingly beautiful. Why?"

Yingtai became more apprehensive. "What made you feel so certain that all these gifts are from Shanbo?"

"Who else could they be from?" Yinxin asked.

"Something is very wrong here." Yingtai went to the window where the noise from the sitting room became louder.

"Shanbo does not come from a rich family. How could he afford this much jewelry?"

"Yes, you are right. Sijiu used to tell me that Master Liang didn't have much money or material possessions, only some books." Yinxin's excitement died down as she began to think.

"Besides, Shanbo could not have managed to come today even if he had been most efficient in leaving school and getting home. And it is impossible for him to get so many expensive gifts for his parents could not afford to even send him money for his education!"

Yingtai said to herself, getting more and more worried, "My mother promised to talk to my father about Shanbo, but she has not gotten back to me for so long. This is unlike her."

A chill came over her.

"Something must be going on behind my back," she concluded. A heavy sense of uneasiness arose in her.

Yingtai decided that she could not just wait there passively. She would go and talk to her parents after dinner.

That afternoon Yingtai was restless. She found it impossible to think of anything except the whereabouts of Shanbo. By then, she knew that the presents could not come from him and that was definitely a very bad sign. Who could have sent those things? Her father must have allowed this to happen.

What if that was the case and her father would not change his mind? Would she change her mind? She knew she could not. Then what would follow?

She knew she was firm in her choice. She only wanted to marry Shanbo and no one else. She would do everything to make that happen.

CHAPTER 14

WHEN SHE APPEARED for dinner that day, Yingtai said to her parents, "I would like to have a talk with you after dinner."

Her parents looked at each other and nodded in agreement. They could tell that Yingtai had known or sensed something. She had never spoken to them so abruptly before.

No one breathed a word during dinner, which added to the tension.

"Something is going on and I am afraid it has to do with me." Yingtai initiated the conversation with restraint after dinner. "It appears that I am the only person left in the dark."

"Yingtai, we have great news for you, but it is not about Shanbo," Mrs. Zhu started in a guilty voice. "It was a little too late when I brought the subject of Shanbo up with your father." Afraid that Yingtai could not take too much at one time, she chose her words very discreetly.

Though more or less prepared, Yingtai was dumbfounded at this.

"What does 'a little too late' mean?" her voice faltered.

Mrs. Zhu was too fearful to say anything. She looked at her husband for help.

"To tell you the truth, Wencai Ma, an excellent young man, the son of Taishou Ma, was introduced to me by a matchmaker the other day," Gongyuan Zhu said, trying to ignore Yingtai's reaction.

"He is handsome, intelligent and rich. I am convinced that he will be a good match for you. So I gave him the affirmative answer for marriage. He and his father were so delighted that they lost no time in sending betrothal presents." Seeing Yingtai's face go pale, he added, "Yingtai, trust me. This is the best thing I could ever do for you. You will have a much better life than the one you could ever have with this Shanbo person."

Tears rolled down Yingtai's cheeks. Her ears were ringing, blocking out what Gongyuan Zhu was saying.

"I don't care about that stranger. Let him have his good life with somebody else. I want only Shanbo. Don't even try to change my mind. I know what I am talking about." Yingtai hissed from between clenched teeth.

"Yingtai, my child, please calm down. We are not saying Shanbo is not good enough. We have not even met him yet." Mrs. Zhu tried to console her.

"He will come. I am sure he will. In only a few more days," Yingtai cried out.

"But Wencai Ma has already come and given you the gifts. From now on, there will be no more mention of this Shanbo person!" Gongyuan Zhu said forcefully.

"No!" Yingtai said disregarding his authority. "Shanbo did come earlier. We had a matchmaker too. And he has my jade butterflies to prove it."

Gongyuan Zhu almost laughed, "You are a woman. You cannot hire yourself a matchmaker like that. Anyway, what do the jade butterflies prove? They were yours to begin with, never his. You two simply cannot decide if you can marry. That is not the way things are done."

"That is the way things are done for me!" Yingtai challenged him again.

"How dare you speak to me like that? Don't forget I am your father!" Gongyuan Zhu finally lost his temper. "Is that what an education did for you?"

"I always respect you, Father. But you just did something disrespectful of me. How could you make such an important decision without first consulting me?" Yingtai argued.

Gongyuan Zhu shook with anger. "Who told you that I should consult you for ... for that matter. You, you get out of this room this minute! Get out!"

"Fine. I just want you to know that I am not going to have anything to do with that stranger." She dashed out of the room.

The next morning, Yingtai did not go to breakfast. In fact, she did not even get up. It was unlike the tricks she used to play when she wanted something. Looking back, she felt she could afford to lose any battle she had had with her father, but not this time. She had to win this one. If not, she saw no purpose in life.

Mrs. Zhu came to see her after breakfast.

"If you are here to talk about that stranger, I am not available for conversation," Yingtai said in distress.

"Yingtai, I don't want to see you fight with your father again. Besides, it is not the way to get what you want. As he said, he did it for your own good."

"What he thinks is good for me is not what I think is good for me."

"If you think it out, Wencai is a pretty good choice. He is talented, and he has money."

"I am not interested in his money. I only want to be with someone who loves me and whom I love. Did I not make myself clear yesterday? If I cannot marry Shanbo, I would rather be a spinster for the rest of my life."

"That won't do. What would happen to you after we die? Just listen to me this once. Your father is not likely to change his mind. You must stop thinking about Shanbo."

"How can I? I promised I would wait for him. Why should I change my mind? I belong to him now and I will still be his until the day I die," Yingtai said firmly.

"Perhaps you need more time to think. Meanwhile, we will wait to see whether Shanbo even comes."

Yingtai burst into tears after Mrs. Zhu had left. She knew how things were. She knew it would be a disgrace to accept gifts from someone and then break off the engagement by sending the things back, especially to a family like the Mas. She was sure she would not marry Wencai Ma, but the possibility of sharing her life with Shanbo was becoming more remote. Parental authority regarding marriage, the influence of the Ma family in the area, and the old traditions—all this was going to cloud her future with Shanbo.

It seemed Yingtai had dropped from heaven into hell. She refused to accept the prospect that Shanbo could only live in her memory from now on. How would he react to this when he came to propose? She could not bear the idea of hurting him.

She thought of eloping with Shanbo when he came for her. But where could they go? Worse yet, since her father had accepted gifts from the Ma family, it would be in their interest to track her down. She knew Taishou Ma was a very powerful man. They would get caught before they could even escape because the entire territory was under his control. If that happened, Shanbo's life would be in danger.

Despair was eating at Yingtai's heart bit by bit. She lay there motionless, letting the pain of hopelessness torment her into a state of numbness. Tears kept streaming down her face, soaking her pillow. Yinxin sat next to her bed in quiet desperation, weeping and keeping her company.

Late in the afternoon, Yingtai gathered herself up and tried to resume her needlework. With tears in her eyes, she looked at the butterflies with a new perspective. As needles ran in and out of the cloth, Yingtai cheered up a little. This was not the end yet. She could work harder on her father. The worst scenario would be that she would hang on there to see what could be done next. If her father forced her to marry Wencai Ma, she would threaten to kill herself. She knew her father would not go so far as to let that happen. If she won that battle, she could wear her parents' patience out and make them agree to let her marry Shanbo.

Yingtai smiled to herself as she thought of this new approach, her fingers moving nimbly with the needle. Finally she completed the wings of the butterflies. She held the cloth away from her to take a better look. The wings were perfect: they were still, but one could almost feel the life and vigor within them. These would be the wings that took her and Shanbo to the free land.

She wept silently, but this time they were tears of joy and hope in a time of despair.

CHAPTER 15

IT TOOK SHANBO and Sijiu several days to walk back home. They arrived on a late afternoon. Shanbo spotted his father sitting at the door of the house looking at passers-by. They walked on and stopped in front of old Master Liang, who stared at him with disbelief for a few minutes.

"Shanbo! Is that you?" cried Old Master Liang.

"Yes, Father. I am back." Shanbo bowed to his father.

"How are you, old Master Liang?" Sijiu went up and bowed too.

"What a pleasant surprise!" Old Master was exhilarated. "Come on in. Your mother will be very happy to see you."

Mrs. Liang was making dinner as they walked in. She half closed her eyes to look at the visitors.

"How are you, Mother?"

"Oh, my, is that you Shanbo?" She jumped up like a child, and held Shanbo tight by the hand. "Why have you come back unannounced?"

"There was no time for that. It was an emergency."

"What is wrong?" Mrs. Liang was alarmed.

"Nothing is wrong. In fact, something is wonderful. I will tell you the whole story later." Shanbo put down the luggage, panting a little with excitement.

After dinner, the family continued to sit at the table in the candlelight. Shanbo slid into a hallucination for a moment. He could see Yingtai sitting opposite him! What a difference a few days could make: he was sitting with his parents, and Yingtai, once again living as a woman, must also be sitting with her parents at home.

"So tell us about your time at school." Old Master Liang's words shook Shanbo from his illusion.

Shanbo started the long story by describing how he met Yingtai on the way to Hangzhou, how they settled in the same apartment, how they became brothers, how they read at the same table by the same candlelight, and above all, how Yingtai insisted on sharing expenses with him so that he could continue his schooling for another year and a half.

"What a great friend! Friends like these are few and far between," Old Master Liang commented.

"You are so fortunate, Shanbo, that you found such a wonderful brother for yourself," remarked Mrs. Liang.

"That is only half of the story. Yingtai was called home about a few days ago. He left me with a great surprise. Mrs. Zhou told me that Yingtai was really a woman disguised in man's clothing! She did this because it was the only way she could leave home and be accepted at school!"

Both Old Master and Mrs. Liang were too shocked to say a word.

Shanbo looked at them with understanding, remembering his own reaction to the disclosure.

"Well, before I had known the truth, I walked Yingtai part way home. Right before we said good-bye, she mentioned that she had a twin sister who looked exactly like her. She suggested that I should go and visit her father and make a proposal of marriage for the sister."

"What did you say?" Mrs. Liang's eyes lit up.

"What else could I say? Yingtai comes from a good family, and her sister had read a lot at home. Besides, this was a way Yingtai and I could stay close to each other."

Old Master Liang nodded in acquiescence.

"It was after I returned to school that Mrs. Zhou asked to talk with me. She gave me a jade butterfly that Yingtai had left for me." Shanbo could not hide his happiness at this, his face glowing in the dim room. "She also left words that she would not want to marry any one but me."

"But what about the twin sister?" Mrs. Liang was concerned.

"There is no twin sister! Yingtai was acting as a go-between for herself!" said Old Master Liang. "Don't you understand, silly woman?"

"Oh, what a brave girl! Shanbo, when are you going to propose? You had better hurry before her parents promise her to somebody else." Mrs. Liang now had a new reason to worry.

"Yingtai wants me to go to her home within the month. This is only the ninth day since she left. I promised Yingtai that I would go to see her father as soon as I could. Of course, I was thinking of asking her father for the hand of her non-existent sister. I hope you don't mind my making this decision without consulting you beforehand."

"We don't mind at all, especially since Yingtai seems to be such a special woman to you," said Old Master Liang.

"Go whenever you think the time is right," said Mrs. Liang.

"But we don't have much money to buy decent betrothal gifts for Yingtai. Will this impair your chance of getting her parents' permission for the marriage?" Old Master Liang worried.

"Yingtai has already said that this would not be a problem. Yingtai is not the type that judges the value of a person by the size of his moneybag. She values love and friendship more," Shanbo assured him.

"She is truly a wonderful woman. You are so lucky, Shanbo," said the happy Mrs. Liang.

The knowledge that Yingtai had absented herself for three meals in a row irritated and disturbed Gongyuan Zhu. He wanted her to be happy. He could understand how sad she might be with all that had transpired. But she was too young and naive to understand that she really did not have a choice in the matter. Saying no to the Ma family would bring total disaster upon the Zhu family. Besides, he rationalized, Wencai Ma really did seem to be the better man for her.

Gongyuan Zhu began to feel sorry that he had ordered Yingtai out of the room the night before. He sent for Yinxin to find out how Yingtai was doing.

"She stays in bed all the time, but does not sleep. She will not eat. And she cries incessantly."

Gongyuan Zhu sighed, "Has she said anything to you?"

"Not much, except that she will not marry anyone but Master Liang."

Gongyuan Zhu sighed again, "What a stupid thing to say!" He started pacing in the room. "When she feels better, tell her to come and see me."

Yinxin went back to Yingtai and told her that Master Zhu was troubled and inquired about her.

"He wants you to go and see him when you feel better."

"I will never feel better." Yingtai got up from the bed. "I had best go and see him now to find out what can be done."

"Father," Yingtai addressed Gongyuan Zhu with distant politeness.

"You have not eaten?"

"No."

"This is not good."

"I know."

"Tell me, what will make you eat again?"

Yingtai looked at her father in surprise. "Do you want to hear the truth?"

Gongyuan Zhu nodded.

"Return the engagement gifts to the Ma family."

"That is a ridiculous thing to say!" Gongyuan Zhu burst out. "I have never heard of such a thing in my life!" he reiterated.

"I know."

Somehow, the fact that Yingtai did not work herself into a big argument with him scared Gongyuan Zhu. That was not like Yingtai. He controlled his fury and said in a softer voice, "The Ma family is too powerful for us. We would get ourselves into big trouble if I rejected their offer."

"I understand."

"Try to cheer up. Wencai Ma and Taishou Ma like you. They will be kind to you. And you will have a good life there."

He went over to his desk, and took out a paper.

"Look, this is a sample of Wencai Ma's writing. You can see for yourself that he is rather gifted."

"Father, I want to make myself perfectly clear for the last time," Yingtai said with restrained sadness. "I am not interested in anything concerning Wencai Ma. He can keep his writing and all his worldly possession to himself. I don't want to hear his name mentioned in front of me ever again. Shanbo is the only man I love. If I cannot have him, I don't want anyone else. If I am forced to marry Wencai Ma, I would prefer to die."

Gongyuan Zhu turned pale as he heard Yingtai's statement.

"You are not giving me much choice. You are not giving yourself much of a choice either," he said, his long beard shaking slightly.

"That is because I know there is only one choice for me. I will marry Shanbo and no other."

Yingtai's eyes were full of tears again. She stared at the floor, letting the familiar feeling of desperation creep up and engulf her.

CHAPTER 16

SHANBO FOUND HIMSELF standing in front of the Zhu house after a long walking trip. He and Sijiu literally ran part of the way, then spent the bulk of the time climbing up and down the mountains to the Zhu Village. Driven by an unknown urge, Shanbo let his feet take over, walking faster than ever before. He could not wait to see Yingtai again.

Now that he was right in front of Yingtai's home, he was suddenly seized by fear. This visit would decide his and Yingtai's future. What would be waiting for him?

"Master Liang, are we going to knock?" Sijiu asked.

"Perhaps we should check one more time to make sure that this is the right house." The impending meeting was just too important and he must make sure that nothing went wrong. All of a sudden, Shanbo was overcome by nervousness, and manufactured excuses to postpone the inevitable.

"It cannot be wrong. According to Master Zhu, no, Miss Zhu, the house is the most conspicuous in the village, and is the only one that has six willow trees in front of it, three on each side. This house fits the description."

Shanbo shook his head a little to come out of his undesirable state of mind.

"Oh, sure. Let me get my breath back before we knock. It has been a tiring trip."

This was true. He did feel tired, exhausted in fact.

An old man came to the gate to answer the door soon after Sijiu had knocked.

"My name is Shanbo Liang. I'm here to see Master Gongyuan Zhu."

"I am afraid he is not home today. He left on a trip yesterday."

Shanbo was both disappointed and relieved. Anyway, this would give him some time to talk things over with Yingtai so that the proposal would go well.

"In that case, I would like to see Miss Yingtai Zhu."

The old man looked doubtful. How could Miss Zhu have a male visitor?

"We studied together in Hangzhou," explained Shanbo. "I would like to see Mrs. Zhu also."

"Oh, I understand. Please come in."

The man led them to the sitting room. He went to the garden to report to Mrs. Zhu who was taking a stroll there.

"There is a Shanbo Liang here to see Master Zhu. I told him Master is away, but he said he would like to meet you and Miss."

"Where is he now?" Mrs. Zhu stopped walking and asked. She became uneasy. This would definitely create new tension between Yingtai and her father.

"In the sitting room."

Hurrying to the sitting room, Mrs. Zhu thought it a good thing that her husband was not home. She knew he would not let the two young people meet, but she could not and would not do that to her daughter. She was about to send someone to inform Yingtai, then changed her mind and went straight to Yingtai's room herself.

Yingtai was standing by the window in deep thought.

"Yingtai, Shanbo is here!"

Yingtai's face radiated, but was soon darkened by the shadow of sadness. Filled with mixed feelings of joy and grief, she said, "I must see him immediately."

"Wait a minute! You had better see him in man's clothing. And I think you should tell him about the engagement yourself."

"Why? Has he not seen enough of me in man's clothes? I want him to see me as a woman," Yingtai protested.

Mrs. Zhu did not insist. Yingtai had already suffered too much.

Frantically, Yingtai searched for clothes. She wanted to look her best for Shanbo. Who knew how many more times they would see each other? Tears rushed to her eyes as she dressed herself.

Meanwhile, Mrs. Zhu went to greet Shanbo. She smiled to the handsome young man clad in blue.

"How are you, Mrs. Zhu?" Shanbo stood up and bowed to her.

"I am very well, thank you. And how are you?"

Mrs. Zhu liked Shanbo instantly. Shanbo was still dressed like a student. His clothes were not made of expensive material, but they showed very fine needlework in the embroidered part at the bottom of the long gown. Plus, he had a very refined and courteous manner. If only he had come a few days earlier! This cultured young man would have had a better chance to become her prospective son-in-law.

"I am fine. This is Sijiu, my servant." Shanbo signaled Sijiu to bow to Mrs. Zhu.

When they sat down, Mrs. Zhu asked, "Are you just passing through town?"

"No, this is a special visit," Shanbo said a little absent-mindedly. Where was Yingtai?

Mrs. Zhu seemed to have read his mind, and said, "My daughter will be here in no time." Her heart ached to see the anxious look upon his face.

As she said this, Shanbo saw a familiar looking girl in female servant's clothes walk into the room.

"Oh, I cannot believe this!" exclaimed Sijiu. "Is that you Yinxin?" He stepped forward to observe Yinxin. She was in light yellow trousers, with a light yellow shirt that ran down to her knees. Her hair was parted into two braids, a hair band running across the top of her head, completed by two little jewels. She had become a woman of some charm just by changing into woman's clothes.

Shanbo made a gesture to remind him of his manners.

Sijiu checked himself and apologized.

"Hello, Yinxin," he started again politely.

"How are you, Master Liang?" Yinxin dropped a courtesy to Shanbo. She turned around and said, "Miss Zhu is here."

Shanbo's eyes shone. A young woman was walking gracefully toward him. She was wearing a pink shirt and a beige skirt, her hair held back with a tiara of jewels. Her face was lightly made up, and her eyes were radiant with rapture. This is no doubt a beautiful female version of Brother Yingtai he knew so well!

Before Shanbo got over his amazement, Yingtai had come close to him. She dropped a curtsy.

"How are you, Shanbo?"

"I am fine, just fine."

Dazzled by Yingtai's beauty, Shanbo could scarcely complete his end of the ritual, only remembering to bow.

Observing the exchange between the two, Mrs. Zhu could not help thinking that they would make a great couple. Softened by the idea, she decided to give them some private time together, though it was forbidden by tradition.

"If you would excuse me, Shanbo, I would like to leave for the time being to take care of some other business," she said.

Shanbo stood up and bowed politely. "Please go ahead."

Mrs. Zhu got up and said, "Yingtai, come with me for a minute."

"You can have a good talk with him since your father is not here. But try to make it short and watch your behavior. Your reputation will be ruined if the Ma family gets wind of this meeting. I will ask the chef to make a good meal. Shanbo will have to leave after lunch. Your father could come back any time after that."

Yingtai was grateful, but did not like what her mother said.

"I don't care what the Ma family thinks of me. All I care is I don't disappoint Shanbo. I told you he would come for me," she said, trying to stop her tears.

"I told you all that with good intentions," Mrs. Zhu said sorrowfully.

Yingtai gave her mother an appreciative look, unable to speak.

"Calm down. You don't want Shanbo to see you like this," said Mrs. Zhu sympathetically.

Yingtai restrained herself, wiping her tears carefully. When she went back to the sitting room, she managed to plaster on a false smile. Yinxin and Sijiu were talking in a low voice in one corner, Shanbo was standing by his chair, making no attempt to hide his eagerness.

"This is not a good place to talk. Come with me to my study."

Shanbo followed quietly. He had so many things to say to Yingtai, but words failed him.

"Yinxin, you can show Sijiu around in the garden."

"Come on, Sijiu," Yinxin jumped up jubilantly.

When they were gone, Yingtai led the way through the garden to her study.

Shanbo noticed that the peonies were at their best. Immediately, Yingtai's words about giving him all the peonies in her garden rang in his ears. From that moment, Shanbo began to see the future with Yingtai very clearly. He became very animated.

Shanbo walked up with Yingtai to a second floor room. He knew this was her study. Three bookshelves stood by the wall, two musical instruments were on the other side of the room. A desk was in the middle with a few books, writing brushes, Chinese ink stick and inkstone on it. All three windows were open, and the leaves of the tall trees crowded into their openings, providing cool shade to the room.

"What a great place for a study," Shanbo sat down by the desk. "It is inspiring to talk in it too."

"However, such a chance to talk is a luxury for us," Yingtai said sadly.

"Why are you looking so gloomy? Are you not happy to see me?" Shanbo could detect the depression in Yingtai, but was not able to see the reason.

"Why didn't you come to see me earlier?" Yingtai asked reproachfully.

"I am already here earlier than you asked me to come. I missed you so much! I have been so excited. How stupid of me not to know you were a woman! I had thought that nothing would be better than brotherhood between us. I still cannot believe that we can look to sharing our lives together forever." Shanbo was almost out of breath with excitement. "You cannot imagine how fast we walked. We ran most of the way until we tired ourselves out."

Yingtai was very touched. She turned around to wipe off her tears.

"What is the matter?" Shanbo became more worried than confused.

"You came too late!" Yingtai burst out crying.

"What do you mean?" Shanbo became agitated.

"A few days ago, a matchmaker came to introduce my father to the son of a rich and powerful family. My father could not say no for fear of their reprisal."

"He could not say no. But did he say yes?" Shanbo lost his ability to comprehend.

"Yes, he did." Yingtai breathed out the words in a very low voice as if they could crush Shanbo if she said them too loudly.

"They have ... already sent ... the betrothal presents." Yingtai could barely hear her own voice, as she punctuated the sentence with weeping.

Shanbo's face turned very pale. A chill shot through his body and his chest had a dull pain as if someone had hit him hard. He saw stars and his body began to tremble. He held on to the desk instinctively.

"Shanbo! Shanbo! Are you all right?" Not strong enough to support him, Yingtai shouted into the garden, "Sijiu, come here quickly!"

Sijiu rushed upstairs followed by Yinxin. They helped to move Shanbo to Yingtai's bed.

Shanbo was sweating all over. He came to a few minutes later and jumped out of bed. Staring into Yingtai's eyes, he cried out hysterically, "You made a promise to me, and I came for you as soon as I could. How could you have let this happen?"

"I am so sorry, Shanbo," Yingtai said sobbing. "The whole thing was completely beyond my control."

"Since you are marrying someone else, I guess there is nothing I can do or say here. I had better get on my way." Shanbo said coldly, repressing his tears.

"You cannot leave me like this! We have not even talked. Please don't be angry with me. I have been fighting with my parents. I told them that I would not marry anyone but you. If they try to force me to, I will choose to die!"

At this, Shanbo recovered a little, but his face was still as pale as a sheet.

"If you can choose death, you can certainly choose life. Come away with me and we will set up a new home far from here." As he made this suggestion, Shanbo began to see some hope. He fixed his eyes on Yingtai to look for a positive response.

"You have no idea how much influence the Ma family has here. I have thought about the same thing. But they will catch us before we get anywhere. They may even find an excuse to kill you," Yingtai said helplessly.

"Then I shall sue them. They cannot force you to marry."

"Shanbo, you sound so childish. Those working for the government are all connected to the family. They will certainly protect the Ma family over you."

"Are you saying there is nothing we can do about this? Is there no justice in this world?" Shanbo asked in despair.

"Listen to me, Shanbo. I can at least do this for you: under no circumstances will I agree to go to the Ma family."

Yingtai became very determined. "If I can hang on like this long enough, I am sure we can work something out."

Shanbo became very pessimistic. "But are we in a position to fight against these powerful people? Is there any hope that we will win?"

Yingtai did not respond to that. "Do you still have my jade butterflies?" she asked.

"Yes, I carry them in the pocket closest to my heart."

"Please keep them. And I have one more thing for you." Yingtai went to the embroidery room to get her needlework and came back with the tapestry on which she had sown the butterflies.

"This is the very thing that kept me going when we were not together. I started it because it was the only thing that meant something to me. When I learned about the engagement, it was the only thing that gave me back some hope. I have named the butterflies Shanbo and Yingtai. They are the symbol of our free spirit."

Shanbo took the embroidery with excitement.

"Yingtai, this will never be apart from me. As long as I have it on me, I know we are together," he uttered with difficulty. Something heavy on his chest was bothering him.

"You look awful! Are you ill?" Yingtai felt his forehead, "I think you have a fever."

"I don't feel well. I must leave. I cannot fall ill here." Shanbo rose, his eyes fixed on Yingtai, but his feet unwilling to move.

"Please don't go yet. My mother has asked the chef to prepare lunch for you."

"No, I cannot stay for lunch. I must go before I collapse," Shanbo said in a weak voice.

Yingtai was heartbroken. "I cannot allow you to leave like this. You need a doctor. You need a good rest."

"No, not yet, not here. It would not be appropriate. I must leave," Shanbo insisted, wheezing.

Yingtai was torn by hopelessness. Tears washed down her face. She knew Shanbo would not stay. She knew she might never see him again if she let him out of her sight. She could not tell Shanbo enough that she would never succumb to the Ma family.

"Shanbo, let us share a drink before you go. I want to tell you one last thing."

Yinxin flew out of the door to get some wine. Sijiu followed her downstairs.

A faint smile came to Shanbo's colorless face. "You have learned to drink. I still remember the first time when you got drunk."

Yingtai smiled in tears. "That was the first time you held me. I always wondered if you would have done the same had you known I was a woman," she said daringly, knowing this was totally unacceptable for a woman to say.

"I would probably not have. But I am happy that I did not know then. I have been going over all of our most intimate moments, turning Brother Yingtai to a woman. I spent the last few nights at the school in your bed. That was the closest I could get to you. Those memories and fantasies will keep me company until we can be together forever."

Yinxin and Sijiu came back with a jar of wine. Sijiu poured each of them a bowl.

Shanbo raised his bowl. "Let us drink a toast. Yingtai, please thank your mother for me."

Yingtai raised her bowl. "Let us drink to our union. Alive or dead, we will be inseparable!"

Shanbo raised his bowl higher, "Yingtai, I take your word. If I die before our union, I should be able to close my eyes in peace and happiness thinking of what you just said." Having said that, he gulped down the bowl of wine.

Yingtai gulped down the wine in one gulp too. "This is very sweet wine. Why don't I feel sweet?" She burst into tears. Grabbing the jar from Sijiu, she poured herself another bowl, and then filled Shanbo's bowl.

Shanbo did not say a word, but gulped down the second serving with repressed grief. He was instantly choked and began coughing violently. Something red rushed out of his mouth. He was coughing blood!

Yingtai was terrified. She patted Shanbo on his back.

"How are you feeling? It is all my fault. I have caused you so much harm." She stamped on the floor. "Let me send for a doctor for you."

"Don't bother," Shanbo struggled to sit straight. "It happened ... because I could not handle ... the blow of your engagement. And I am very ... very tired from the trip. Now that I know your ... how you feel about us, I will come to terms ... with things. I will be fine. Trust me," Shanbo stumbled the words out comfortingly.

Yingtai looked at him in doubt. "Are you sure?"

Shanbo nodded. Yinxin gave him some water to gargle.

"Now I must be going." Shanbo got up with Sijiu's help.

Yingtai became very quiet. She was still holding the bowl of wine. She stared into it for a long time, then raised her head high and drained the bowl with one swallow.

"Let me walk you to the gate." Yingtai rose slowly. Noting that her movements were not very steady, Yinxin tried to offer her help, but Yingtai refused.

Shanbo made for the door. His steps were wobbly. Yingtai followed him closely for fear he would fall. She also told Yinxin to prepare two horses.

Shanbo stopped under a big willow tree on one side of the garden. Yingtai knew he must be thinking of the first time they had met. She looked up, "Promise me that you will meet me again under a willow tree."

"I would, if I believed I could get over this sickness. But I have a feeling that I am coming down with something serious. Who knows whether I will recover at all," Shanbo said in a weak voice, looking at Yingtai with the saddest look. "I may never be able to meet you under a willow tree again."

"If that happens, I will surely join you in the grave. Do you remember that we agreed to share the same grave?" Yingtai asked him without thinking.

"Are you sure? I know there is a cemetery located in Huqiao county about halfway between our two homes. I would like my final resting place to be there," Shanbo said.

"Then I will be buried there too. If you go first, put my name down on the tombstone next to yours. I will join you as soon as I can. You will not be alone for long." Yingtai said. Somehow a smile came to her face. "Now you know that we will be together till the end of time, no matter what."

A faint smile came to Shanbo's pale face.

"But, please! Please give me some hope. Please give us some hope while we are still alive!" Yingtai begged.

They walked through the garden to get to the gate. Neither of them was walking too sure-footedly, Shanbo from the sickness, Yingtai from the wine.

"I want to hold you," Yingtai said boldly.

"No, you must not risk it. Someone may be watching us. It would ruin your reputation. The Ma family ..."

"What do I care about the Ma family?!" Yingtai said defiantly, taking hold of Shanbo's arm. "I have nothing to do with them. Besides, you are sick, and I want to help you."

Shanbo was embarrassed. This would be a disgrace for Yingtai. He tried to withdraw his arm, but Yingtai's grip was very firm. She then slipped her hand into his.

Shanbo gave up. He had no strength left and it took everything he had simply to feel Yingtai's hand. A wave of warmth went through his palm to all parts of his body, giving him life, life that came from Yingtai.

Shanbo steadied himself. "I love this garden. It is good to see the place where you grew up. I feel I know you much better." He looked up at the sky. "What a nice day. How can something so sad happen during such bright sunlight?"

"The sun looks great now, but it will set by late afternoon. It seems to be symbolic of our relationship," Yingtai said sadly.

They walked over the stone bridge. Yingtai saw Shanbo panting a lot so she made him stop and lean against one of the stone pillars. Shanbo closed his eyes and opened his mouth for air. When he opened his eyes, he saw the blossoming lotus flowers in the pond.

"Look at the lotus flowers. When they are gone, they will produce lotus seeds." He looked at Yingtai. "They have a good beginning and a good ending. We had a good beginning too, why can't we have a good ending?"

"Please, Shanbo, don't get so discouraged. We can have a good ending if we make an effort." Yingtai tried to sound positive.

Neither spoke any more. They walked on, supporting each other, passing on restrained passion to each other through their joined hands.

Finally, they stopped at the gate. Yinxin and Sijiu were waiting outside.

Shanbo gave Yingtai's hand a final grip with all his might and let go. They looked at each other through tearful eyes, unable to say a word.

The gatekeeper came to tell Yingtai that her mother wanted her back in the house.

Sijiu helped Shanbo onto Yingtai's Dark Red to ride, and got on the other horse himself.

The horses set off on their journey. Shanbo and Yingtai never took their eyes away from each other until the gatekeeper made Yinxin push Yingtai back into the house.

CHAPTER 17

MRS. ZHU WAS waiting for Yingtai in the sitting room.

"You went too far with Shanbo," she said with a solemn look on her face.

"He was sick. He was coughing blood!" Yingtai argued.

"You could have asked Sijiu to help. You are a young woman who is going to be someone else's bride soon. If your father knew, I would be in trouble for allowing you to have seen Shanbo!"

"Who says I will be someone else's bride?"

"Yingtai, you have got to come to terms with reality."

"The reality is that I will not marry anyone except Shanbo."

"Yingtai, please don't do this to us," Mrs. Zhu softened. "I could see that Shanbo is a very nice young man and I am sorry for him. It is unfortunate that you cannot marry the boy your heart desires. But please trust your father and me. We would not have given consent to the Ma family if we did not think you would have a good life there."

"I know I cannot do anything about it. But I can choose to die rather than marry that Wencai Ma. Mother, I don't see any point in discussing this any more. I am exhausted. I need to go back to my room."

"Don't speak this way, Yingtai." Mrs. Zhu's face turned white. "Wait till your father comes home."

Shanbo had to lay his upper body across the horse. He was feeling hot and cold, but his mind was clearer than ever. Heavy with regret and disillusionment, he blamed himself for what had happened. Things would have been different had he found out earlier that Yingtai was a woman. Had he gone to Yingtai's father with his proposal before going home, he could be preparing for his wedding to Yingtai right now.

Drawn helplessly by the horse, Shanbo was disheartened to find out how powerless he was. He could not do anything to protect Yingtai from the Ma family; he did not even have the strength to walk, Shanbo was overcome with self-anger. Something rushed up his throat. He opened his mouth and several mouthfuls of blood came out. He passed out.

Sijiu was horror-stricken. He stopped the horses and cried out anxiously, "Master Liang! Master Liang! Please hang on there. We will be home soon!" He burst into tears of fright.

Shanbo came to, his head hanging over one side of Dark Red. "Don't worry. I will be all right."

When they got home, Shanbo was more dead than alive. Sijiu had to drag him to his room and he dropped to bed in depletion.

Mrs. Liang was stunned to see her son coming back a different person. Frantically, she made Shanbo some hot tea. Old Master Liang stood in dismay by the door. "What happened?" he kept asking.

Sijiu helped Shanbo drink some tea, after which Shanbo was able to speak a bit.

"Don't worry. I think it is simply a bad cold." Though weak from physical exhaustion, Shanbo was sober enough not to let his parents worry about him. "I will be fine after a good night's sleep."

"Are you sure?" his parents asked in unison.

Shanbo eyes were already closed and he fell into sleep again.

Sijiu told them briefly what had happened during the day.

"So Yingtai is going to marry someone else," Mrs. Liang said mechanically.

"There is nothing we can do about it. Shanbo was giving it too much hope. We are too poor for Yingtai," Old Master Liang concluded.

"No, it was not her choice. She said she would not marry anyone except Master Liang," Sijiu explained.

"Then why has Shanbo fallen so sick so suddenly?" asked Mrs. Liang.

"It must have been a heavy blow for him," said Old Master Liang. "I can see that he really loves Yingtai."

"Let us pray that he gets well soon," said Mrs. Liang.

Sijiu slept next to Shanbo's bed that night. Shanbo was very restless and disturbed in his sleep. Yingtai kept coming into his dreams. All the time, she walked toward him. Just as he held out his arms to touch her, she would back off and fade into distance. Shanbo was extremely frustrated. He wanted to cry out her name, but could not find his voice.

Once as Yingtai came toward him, another man appeared from nowhere, grabbed her by the waist and took her away. Yingtai struggled to set herself free, but the man was strong and dragged her along.

Shanbo heard her cry "Shanbo! Shanbo! Help ... help!" He went crazy, and ran at full speed to throw himself onto the man, roaring with anger ...

"Master Liang, Master Liang, wake up!" Sijiu's voice was ringing in his ears, but sounded very remote.

Shanbo lay motionless for a while, grateful it was only a bad dream. Sijiu was wiping sweat off his forehead with a towel. Shanbo wanted to say something, but stopped because of a severe sore throat.

"You must have been dreaming, Master Liang."

Shanbo groaned in pain. His head was so heavy that he could not even turn to the side. He was wet all over with sweat ...

The next morning, Shanbo woke up feeling no better. Sijiu was still fast asleep. Shanbo supported himself with his arms and got up slowly. Before he moved a step, a fit of dizziness hit him on the head. Before he could hold on to something, he fell to the floor. Sijiu woke up with a start, and helped him back to bed.

"I feel awful, Sijiu. Would you make me some hot water?" Shanbo asked feebly.

Old Master Liang heard the noise and came in to check.

"Are you better today, Shanbo?"

"I am afraid not. I think I am really very sick."

"I will send Sijiu to get a doctor for you."

"I am afraid that will not help much at all."

"Why?"

"Because I feel defeated. I have no more energy to fight for anything. I am so ashamed of myself because I cannot give any help to Yingtai. I am afraid I cannot be with her until after I die," Shanbo said in a whispering voice.

"Things are usually not as bad as people think," Old Mr. Liang tried to sound upbeat. "When you get well, you will change your mind."

Shanbo shook his head. Mrs. Liang came in with a cup of water. She held up Shanbo's head so that he could drink. Instantly, Shanbo could see himself in his mother's position helping Yingtai when she had the cold. If Yingtai knew he was so sick, she would be doing the same thing for him, Shanbo thought.

A doctor came. He could not say for sure what was wrong with Shanbo, but prescribed some medicine anyway. Two more days passed, yet Shanbo showed no sign of recovery. He threw up everything he ate and drank except for an occasional mouthful of water. Within a very short time, his face became gaunt and his eyes looked sunken. Mrs. Liang was rueful seeing her only son withering away. She spent every day kneeing in front of the small Buddha, bowing and praying with a bunch of burning incense in her hands.

On the third night of his illness, Shanbo called his parents to his bedside.

"I am afraid I may not survive this. I am sorry that I will not have the chance to do all the things I wanted for you."

"Nonsense," said Mrs. Liang, weeping. "You will be fine. You must get well. I cannot continue to live without you."

Old Master Liang said, "Don't be so pessimistic. You are far too young to die." He paused to fight his depression. "I was thinking that Sijiu should pay a visit to the Zhus to return the horses."

Shanbo's face lit up at the mention of that. "Yes, Sijiu should go and tell Yingtai how I am. She must be worried. Help me get up. I will write her a letter."

"You are too weak. Sijiu can tell her how you are," Mrs. Liang persuaded.

"I must write. In fact, I feel better now." Shanbo got up with help from Sijiu. "Yingtai is the only person who can save me."

As Sijiu got the writing brush and ink ready, Shanbo had a bowl of rice.

For the first time in three days, he did not vomit.

Pulling himself together, Shanbo wrote:

Dearest Yingtai,

I am sorry that I frightened you the other day. I was totally unprepared for such bad news. I was so blind in the past and I have been blaming myself for that every day. I wasted so much time. I cannot tell you how regretful I am. I also cannot tell you enough just how much I love you. I was hoping that I could make it all up to you after we got married.

I don't want to live without you. I cannot live without you. A doctor has come, but he has no idea what is wrong with me. You are my only hope, my only reason to live.

Yours always,

Shanbo

Shanbo went over the letter once. "I hope I have made myself clear. I am afraid I cannot check to see whether all the words are correct." He turned to Sijiu. "Make sure Yingtai receives it. She will have the proper medicine for me."

Sijiu was puzzled but did not ask any question. He would leave early the next morning.

Shanbo, energized by the prospect of communicating with Yingtai, looked markedly better than in the past two days. He went back to bed, took out the butterfly embroidery and placed it upon his stomach.

An incredible sensation of union with Yingtai crept over him. He ran his fingers over the stitches. They felt soft like Yingtai's hands. He held up the cloth to admire the needle-work. He did not have a sister and had never played with girls. This was the only piece of embroidery he had ever received from a woman. He put it over his face to smell Yingtai. He even tasted it. It was a bit salty. Yingtai must have cried while she was working on it. He pressed the cloth over his eyes so that his tears melted into hers. By doing that, he believed he had somehow built a connection with her.

He loved her creation. He loved the fact that the butter-flies' wings touched each other. She was trying to build a connection too. He could feel the exultation the butterflies shared in flying away. Yes, they were named after the two of them. Shanbo fondled the smaller one, the little Yingtai in pink. She appeared to be fragile, but there was something about her that convinced him she could survive any storm. "Oh, Yingtai, if only I could fly away with you!" Shanbo thought, his heart aching.

He put the cloth back onto his stomach. Then he took out the two jade butterfly pendants. Holding one in each hand, he tried to imagine that they were still warm from Yingtai's body temperature. Shanbo experienced a strange excitement think-ing that they used to hang close to her heart on her necklace.

He put them close to his heart and he could feel his own heart-beats. Somehow, he could hear a second heart beating and he felt more intimate with Yingtai than ever.

Yingtai was fidgety and nervous the minute Shanbo was out of her sight. She was touched by how strongly he felt for her, yet saddened to see how shattered he was. It was impossible for her not to try talking to her father again even if the effort would be in vain.

She went to her parents' room before dinner. She knew her father had just returned. On approaching the room, she heard her father blaming her mother.

"You should not have let them meet. Yingtai is engaged to someone else. It is degrading for her to meet another young man in private. You ought to have sent that Shanbo Liang away."

"How could I do that? They spent almost three years together. Since they cannot be married to each other, I thought they deserved the opportunity to say good-bye. After all, they had a very close relationship," Mrs. Zhu argued. "You would have liked him if you had met him. It was really quite sad. He was so heartbroken that he threw up blood when he learned of Yingtai's engagement!"

"Well, well, now that he is out of the way, we have to focus on the wedding. It is only several days away. We have got to prepare the dowry for Yingtai. Go talk to her and find out what she likes. She is our only daughter and we must get her things that she really loves."

Yingtai was disgusted by every word her father said. She decided to break into their conversation at this point. She knocked and went in when she was summoned.

"You look so pallid, my child. Are you feeling well?" Gongyuan Zhu asked with genuine concern.

Without a word, Yingtai fell to her knees, sobbing.

"Father, for the sake of your love for your daughter, please free me from the Ma family. Shanbo and I have sworn that we would not marry anyone except each other. Please cancel the wedding and return all the gifts to the Ma family."

Gongyuan Zhu was appalled that Yingtai had talked about her relationship with Shanbo so openly to him. He flew into a fury and exploded.

"You don't know what you are talking about. Your wedding is in a few days and you are still talking about Shanbo Liang and sending back gifts to the Ma family! Do you think this is a child's play? Do you really want to see what nasty things Taishou Ma could do to us? Do you think he would take the humiliation of your giving him back the gifts?"

Yingtai was confounded for a few seconds, then found strength and courage at the thought of Shanbo. She picked herself up from the floor and declared.

"I don't care whether you return the gifts or not. I just will not be available on that day. I will not marry Wencai Ma even if he were the emperor's son. Period!"

"You, you ..." Gongyuan Zhu nearly jumped out of his skin. "How dare you go against my will? Listen to this: you must marry Wencai Ma, whether you like it or not!"

Yingtai became unusually calm when she heard this. She knew that was it. Her father would never change his mind. It was no use trying to plead any more. Seeing a pair of scissors on the desk, she ran and grabbed hold of them. Before anyone could say anything, she cut off a bunch of her hair.

Mrs. Zhu screamed and threw herself onto Yingtai and took the scissors away.

"Don't do such stupid things to yourself!" she pleaded.

"If father refuses to return the gifts, I will cut all my hair off and go to a nunnery!" Holding the shank of the cut hair, she stormed out of the room.

Strangely enough, Yingtai did not find herself very upset this time. She was hoping that her extreme action would be enough of a threat to make her father cancel the wedding. If that did not work, she would seriously consider becoming a nun. She figured that even the nunnery would provide more freedom than staying at home. Hopefully, she could resume a secular life later and marry Shanbo in the future.

Yingtai refused to see her parents for the next three days. She ate very little and shut herself in her room all day long. She spent her time staring into the garden, wild with all kinds of tricks and thoughts, now crying, now smiling to herself. Yinxin grew very worried and tried to distract her, but scarcely succeeded.

On the fourth day after Shanbo's visit, Yinxin was in the garden picking flowers. She knew there was very little she could do to help Yingtai. She was hoping that some flowers in the room could cheer her up a little.

The gatekeeper came to her and said, "Your brother is here to see you."

"My brother?" Yinxin was baffled.

"The one who came with his Master a few days ago."

Yinxin was delirious. It must be Sijiu. He must be sending news about Master Liang. She just wanted to run to the door to meet him. But on second thought, she asked the gatekeeper, "Did anyone else see him?"

"No."

"Could you let him in through the back door? You know, I don't want to run into trouble."

"All right. If anyone asks, I saw no one. I let no one in." The gatekeeper promised.

"Did Master Liang send you here? How is he?" Yinxin asked as Sijiu walked into the garden.

"Yes, he is not very well. I am here to deliver a letter to Miss Zhu," Sijiu said. He looked worried and tired.

Yinxin led Sijiu to Yingtai's study, where Yingtai was sitting with a distant look in her eyes. As soon as she recognized Sijiu, she livened up. "Did Shanbo send you here? How is he?" she asked solicitously.

"He is very sick. He wrote you this letter."

Yingtai grabbed the letter. She read it quickly for the first time, and read it again. On the third reading, she began to cry. "Shanbo, if not for me, you would not have fallen so ill."

"Master Liang said that you had some medicine for him. He said you were the only person who could save his life." Sijiu looked at Yingtai expectantly.

More tears rushed into Yingtai's eyes. "I am afraid I cannot save him."

Sijiu turned gloomy. "Do you have the medicine?"

"You don't understand. He wants to know whether I have managed to change my father's mind. How am I going to tell him that I could not?" She covered her face with both hands and cried. "And worse yet, I cannot even go to see him while he is so sick."

Yinxin and Sijiu exchanged a helpless look.

"Perhaps you can ask Sijiu to take something to Master Liang," Yinxin suggested.

"Yes. You are right. Will you go to the kitchen and ask the chef to gather some tonics while I write the letter? Sijiu, you go with Yinxin to the gatekeeper. He will find you a bed to take a nap in before you go."

Yingtai then set to work. She wrote:

My Dear Shanbo,

I have been worried about you since the very second you left. I wish I could come with Sijiu to see you. I would elope with you if I could, but I told you earlier that it would be out of the question. Things are not any better here. But I want to assure you that I will never give up.

I wish I could go and confront Wencai Ma and tell him in person that I will never marry him. Should the worst happen, be assured that you and I will meet again in the graveyard.

I want you to know that we will be together one way or the other. I am enclosing a lock of my hair in this letter. Keep it close to you, so that I can be with you. I cut the hair to show my parents that I would rather go to the nunnery than marry Wencai Ma. I believe we can find a way to be together if I do go and stay in the nunnery for a while. Please hang on. Somehow and some way, we will meet again soon.

Lovingly,

Your Yingtai

She took the lock of hair from under her pillow and put it in with the letter. She was not as sad any more. Writing the letter had given her a strange tranquility: her life was no longer controlled by others. She knew what she would do and she knew how to do it.

Yinxin came back to tell that the tonics were ready. She went to wake up Sijiu who came to take the letter and say good-bye to Yingtai.

"Please tell Shanbo to endure things for the moment. I was unable to make my father change his mind, but he could not change mine either. Tell him that I will be here for him. When he recovers, we will find a way to meet. The most important thing now is his will to survive."

Sijiu did not seem to understand the situation very well, but promised to pass Yingtai's message on to Shanbo. Yingtai insisted on his riding back on Dark Red, saying Shanbo would be happy to see him back sooner.

CHAPTER 18

SIJIU MADE THE journey back more quickly on Dark Red. As soon as he entered the village, he could see Mrs. Liang standing outside the Liang house, anxiously looking out. Her face lit up when she saw him heading her way.

As Sijiu dismounted the horse, she approached him nervously.

"Shanbo has been asking for you. I think his very life depends on this trip. Did you get the medicine?" she asked with hope.

Sijiu was too heavy-hearted to say anything. He pointed to the tonics and went straight into Shanbo's room. Shanbo was only half awake. He opened his eyes when he heard Sijiu's footsteps.

"Sijiu, is that you?" He propped himself halfway up in the bed. "How was Yingtai? Did she give you the medicine?" He asked in a weak but expectant voice, his face brightening at the mention of Yingtai.

"Master Liang, she wrote you a letter. Would you like to read it first?" Sijiu asked, trying to avoid answering the question.

Shanbo grabbed the letter and held it as if it contained magical properties. He leaned against the wall and began reading. He groaned in anguish and cried, "Poor Yingtai! She is trying so hard to comfort me. She is doing all she can to ensure our future. She has such courage, such strong will power!"

Shanbo read the letter one more time. "What an incredible woman she is! She even wants to confront Wencai Ma!" he commented with awe. "She must be very disappointed with me for being so weak and submissive!"

Shanbo's face was burning as he compared Yingtai's fighting spirit to his own passive acceptance of Yingtai's engagement. "Why do I just succumb to tradition and power? Why do I just accept it without any protest?" Shanbo was abashed by his feeble reaction to the matter so far. He decided that he must do something about it. As he thought of this, he experienced an extraordinary change—all of a sudden, he could stand up and walk almost as usual. "I must do something for Yingtai. I must not let her continue fighting on her own!" he vowed to himself.

"Master Liang! Why are you suddenly looking so much better? Miss Zhu told me that she did not have the medicine you needed," Sijiu cried out in joyful surprise.

"She has done her best. I think it is my turn now," Shanbo said. All the while, he felt strength building in him.

"I think I can eat something now, Sijiu."

Sijiu immediately left the room.

Mrs. Liang came in, wild with rapture.

"Shanbo, are you really feeling better? The Buddha must be answering my prayers. I will bring you a meal this instant!"

"Sijiu, did you say that Yingtai sent along some tonics for me?" Shanbo asked Sijiu.

"Yes, she said they will give you energy." Sijiu looked at Shanbo in disbelief. He could hardly believe his eyes. A miracle seemed to have occurred. Shanbo had gone from being near death's door to relatively good health in a matter of minutes!

Mrs. Liang came in with a large bowl of rice. "Here you are, my son. The sooner you eat this, the better you will feel."

"I feel better already, Mother," Shanbo said. He could still feel the energy level rising in him. He must get better quickly, for he had much to do for Yingtai and for himself.

"Mother, could you also prepare the tonics for me? I will drink them before going to bed tonight," Shanbo said.

After finishing the rice, Shanbo went back to bed. He wanted to have a good rest so that he could store up enough energy for the next day. He was secretly devising a plan and he wanted to be physically strong for it.

He took Yingtai's lock of hair with him to bed. He had given it a good look when he was reading the letter, and he would now hold it close to his heart, as Yingtai had requested. He held it in his hands. It was shining black and felt as tender as Yingtai herself. Shanbo could hardly bear the happiness of having a part of Yingtai so close to him. He caressed it with his lips and face and hoped that Yingtai could somehow feel him doing it.

The lock of hair became very warm in his hands. He put it under his vest over his heart. It stirred something in him, making him feel more manly than ever before. He realized that he loved Yingtai more than ever. Life would lose all its charm and meaning without Yingtai. Since Yingtai was so determined not to marry Wencai Ma and Yingtai's father was unable to return the gifts to the Mas, the only chance to turn the situation around would be to persuade Wencai Ma to give up Yingtai.

By now, Shanbo knew exactly what he would do: he would try to talk Wencai Ma into canceling the engagement. If he were unsuccessful, he would make new plans with Yingtai. He knew that he and Yingtai were meant to be together, if not in this life, then in the next. Shanbo felt inner peace with this.

Later in the evening, Mrs. Liang came in with the tonic soup. "These are excellent tonics. Drink as much as you can. If you can consume it all, it will do you a lot of good," said Mrs. Liang. "Yingtai is such a wonderful woman. She has been so good to you even if she cannot marry you." Mrs. Liang's eyes filled with tears as she said this. "I wish we had more money. Then she could be your bride."

"Mother, please don't say that. I told you that Yingtai does not care about money at all."

"But her father does. If we were richer and more powerful than the other family, he would have returned the gifts to them and accepted ours."

Shanbo was not sure how to respond to his mother's comment.

"Mother, you may be right in some way, but Yingtai is no ordinary woman. While her father fails to be different from other fathers, she is definitely a different daughter. That was how she could attend school and fool every one of us. I know she will not marry Wencai Ma."

"How can you be so sure?" Mrs. Liang was curious.

"Because she told me so and because I know her," Shanbo said with pride.

The tonic soup gave Shanbo a lot of energy. The soothing warmth of the soup put Shanbo into a good sleep. Something magical was definitely happening. His body was working toward a quick recovery for the next day.

The next morning Shanbo got up early and dressed to go out. He still felt a bit dizzy and weak, but far better than he had for the past few days. He went to the dining room where old Mr. Liang and Mrs. Liang were having breakfast. They were ecstatic to see him looking so much better, but were puzzled by the way he was dressed.

"I am going out for the day," Shanbo said.

"Where are you going? No, you must not go out at all. You are still quite weak. You must stay in and rest for a few more days. You have no reason to go out." Mrs. Liang was so eager to keep Shanbo at home that she went to the door to block his exit.

"I have a very good reason to go out. But I am afraid that I cannot tell you at this point. I can only tell you that I simply have to go out. Trust me. This is my life and I must live it my way." Shanbo said firmly, "Don't worry, I will take Sijiu with me. I will take Yingtai's horse too. We will be returning it tomorrow, but I am sure Yingtai would not mind my using it today."

"What can be so important that you have to do it today?" Old Mr. Liang asked.

"Father, I am an adult. I know what I am doing. What I have to do today is really important to me. I will be back late this afternoon," Shanbo said uncompromisingly. "Sijiu, are you ready?"

"I am coming." Sijiu came out of the servant's room right away. "Master Liang, where are we going ?"

Old Mr. Liang and Mrs. Liang both looked at Shanbo, expecting an answer.

"Sijiu, you are not to question me. You are just to follow me," Shanbo said solemnly.

"Please Shanbo, don't go until you are fully recovered," Mrs. Liang pleaded.

"Mother, please don't try to stop me. I may never fully recover. I have always taken your advice in the past, but please allow me this one exception. If anything goes wrong, Sijiu will be able to take care of me. Don't worry, I will be fine. Good-bye."

Shanbo got on Dark Red without another word. He directed Sijiu to climb upon Dark Red with him. He signaled the horse to gallop. Sijiu never saw him so preoccupied and remained silent during the whole trip. After about three hours of riding at top speed, they arrived at the Ma Village. It occurred to Sijiu that Shanbo was going to deal with the Ma family.

"Master Liang, are you sure this is a good idea?" Sijiu could not help asking.

"Of course it is. This is the only possibility for me and for Yingtai. Since Yingtai refuses to marry Wencai Ma in any case, I should let him know. He is an educated man. He may be gentleman enough to let her go."

Sijiu attempted to say something, but Shanbo stopped him. "I know what I am doing. I must support Yingtai in any possible way. I have to do all I can to show her that I am worthy of her love."

The Ma house was about three times larger than the Zhu house. In front of the house, on both sides of the entry gate, stood a pair of stone lions looking fierce and ready to attack.

The walls of the house were very high, giving the house a menacing look. There was an armed guard at the front gate.

Shanbo had deliberately left in the early morning so that he would have a better chance of finding Wencai Ma at home. He went to the guard and asked in a polite manner to see Wencai Ma. The guard went in to report. He came back after a few minutes, followed by a servant, who led Shanbo and Sijiu inside.

Everything in the house seemed to have been made of stone. The floors were paved with quarry stone and the columns were made of marble. The use of this material made the house look rather cold and forbidding. Shanbo could see a portion of the garden. It contained a few displays of flowers but was largely comprised of various sizes of fish ponds with small stone footbridges arching over them and connecting them to each other. He saw a few servants working in the garden, raking the stone paths and feeding the fish.

Sijiu waited outside while Shanbo was taken into an adjacent room. There was no one in the room. Shanbo stood and looked around. The room was larger than it appeared from the outside. It looked like Wencai Ma's study. What made it distinctive was the expensive redwood furniture placed throughout the room. All of this could be Yingtai's if she wanted it, but she had simply turned her back on such wealth.

Shanbo heard footsteps. He turned to the door just in time to see a young man enter the room. He was fairly handsome, dressed like Shanbo in a light gray student gown. He was condescendingly polite as he addressed Shanbo.

"I am Wencai Ma. You are Shanbo Liang?"

Shanbo bowed to him. "I am honored to make your acquaintance. I apologize for coming uninvited."

"Please take a seat," Wencai pointed to a chair as he sat down cross-legged. "What may I do for you?" he inquired.

"I shall be straightforward and tell you the reason for my presence." Shanbo said, "I have heard of your engagement to Yingtai Zhu of the Zhu Village."

"What about it?" Wencai Ma became alert, keen to hear more.

"To be succinct, I am here to inquire whether you would be willing to give her up." Shanbo looked straight into Wencai Ma's face as he said this.

"What are you talking about? Who are you to ask me such a question?" Wencai Ma was becoming hostile.

"This may sound rather unconventional, but I will tell you the whole story ..." Shanbo poured his heart out and told Wencai Ma of how he and Yingtai had met and how they had spent three years together, and how strongly they felt about each other.

"Yingtai had no idea that her father agreed to the proposal from your family. She knows you are a good man, but she desires to honor the commitment she made to me earlier," Shanbo concluded.

"Are you making this up?" Wencai Ma's face changed from disbelief to amazement, then to humiliated anger.

"No, I am speaking the truth in the hope that you will be understanding and compassionate. We would be most grateful if you would agree to cancel your engagement to Yingtai so that we may marry," Shanbo said.

"Ha ha ha ..." Wencai Ma laughed hysterically. "This whole situation is incredible! So, you spent three years together, and you claim you love each other. What is love? Who are you to talk about loving the woman who is my fiancée? If you had wanted to marry her, you should have gone about it in the proper way. First you should have found a matchmaker, then you should have persuaded her father that you were capable of providing his daughter a good life, and finally, you should have sent the family the customary betrothal presents, just like what I have done. I am not the person you should be talking to," Wencai Ma finished angrily.

Shanbo could see that Wencai was in no way ready to give up Yingtai. He tightened his screws.

"Yingtai says that your family background and your future prospects make you a very desirable choice for marriage. She thinks you would find another suitable woman easily. Since we have already pledged our love to each other and vowed that we will marry only each other and no other, it really is to your benefit to kindly let her go. Why would you want a woman who does not want you?"

"Why should I do this? Why should I give up the woman I have chosen? Because you want me to? And you say that she refuses to marry me? Well, I will show her that no one can deny Wencai Ma! If I choose to marry her, she shall be mine. I tell you this: I am really not interested in her any more because of your story. But I am going to marry her anyway, just to prove to you both that it is I, and I only, who get to decide. As soon as we are married, I shall begin looking for a second wife and then perhaps even more. Yingtai will regret making me unhappy and will pay for it the rest of her life. And by making Yingtai miserable, I can make you miserable all the remaining days of your life as well. You should pay heavily for this insulting request of today," Wencai Ma said viciously, with one of his legs twitching with anger.

Shanbo was burning with rage. If Wencai Ma had told him that he admired Yingtai's beauty and talent, and that he could not possibly bring himself to give her up, then he would have found it easier to handle the denial of his request. But Wencai Ma was refusing him out of spite and malice. Shanbo felt an overwhelming urge to punch this petty and vindictive little rich boy.

Yet he suppressed this impulse. He knew that would not help him and Yingtai anyway. He tried in a more tactic way.

"Master Ma, you and I are both educated men. I respect you and I hope you understand why I come to you for help. Is there anything I can do to help change your mind?"

"Let me think ..." Wencai seemed to soften a little bit also. "I do sympathize with you. You must truly be in love with Miss Zhu." He got up and paced back and forth across the room. Shanbo was nervous. He told himself that he would do anything that Wencai Ma would request, if it meant that he could have Yingtai. He looked at Wencai Ma anxiously.

"Well, well, I don't want to make this any harder on you, Shanbo Liang. I think I can settle for this: Get down on your knees and beg me for Yingtai Zhu. If you can do this, she will be yours." He leered at Shanbo, with a wicked smile on his face.

Blood rushed to Shanbo's head. This was the most insulting thing for a man to do and Shanbo could see that Wencai Ma simply wanted to humiliate him. Shanbo was familiar with the saying "A man would rather be killed than be disgraced." How could he allow himself to suffer this disgrace at the whim of Wencai Ma?

Shanbo was shaking with wrath as he struggled with Wencai Ma's request.

"You cannot bring yourself to do it, can you? Your pride is getting in the way, eh? If you love this woman as much as you claim, and if you are so desperate to have her, you should be willing to do everything and anything you can to get her, should you not?" Wencai Ma leered at Shanbo again, wearing a vile smirk.

Without realizing it, Shanbo had bitten into his lower lip. He thought about Yingtai, about her love, her determination, and her fighting spirit. He decided she was more than worthy of this insult to his manhood.

On a resolute action, Shanbo bit hard into his tongue. Blood streamed out of his mouth. He quickly rose and then squarely knelt down before Wencai Ma. He folded his hands into solid fists, and reminded himself that he was doing this for Yingtai.

"Wow, I am truly impressed. It looks as if you are dying to have this woman. Now, beg for her!" Wencai Ma was a little shocked and disappointed by Shanbo's action.

"Please, would you release Yingtai Zhu ..." Shanbo said between his teeth, his mouth full of blood.

"Ha ha ha ha ... and you call yourself a man! Stand up you fool!" He stepped forward to pull Shanbo to his feet. A dizziness crept over Shanbo, making him wobble a little.

"Unfortunately, I have changed my mind. If you believe that Yingtai Zhu is worth suffering this much humiliation for, then she really must be some woman. And if this the case, why would I ever give her up? I have decided to keep her for myself. Sorry to disappoint you."

Shanbo stood in total disbelief, too devastated to say anything.

Wencai Ma started to walk toward the door. "I have other things to attend to now. A servant will be here momentarily to show you out." He turned and gave Shanbo an malicious look.

"Best of luck in the future."

Shanbo was so consumed with rage that he saw red. With a deafening roar, he threw himself at Wencai Ma and spat blood into his face. Wencai Ma gave a loud cry. He pushed Shanbo to the floor and shouted, "Guards! Come and throw this idiot out of my house!"

Instantly, several strong men arrived with clubs. They rushed to Shanbo and showered him with blows. Shanbo was too weak to defend himself against the brutal attack, and he passed out immediately.

Sijiu knew something was terribly wrong when he heard the vociferous roar. Though he was not sure if the cry came from Shanbo, he knew it came from the room where Shanbo was meeting Wencai Ma. Then he saw the guards rushing in with clubs. He knew Shanbo was in serious trouble.

Sijiu looked around anxiously for something he could use to come to Shanbo's rescue. There was nothing around except the rocks in the garden. He ran and grabbed a huge rock that he could wield as a weapon. Armed with it, Sijiu yelled and burst into the room.

Wencai Ma's men, seeing the red-faced Sijiu looking ready to fight them to death, chose to keep their distance and fled from the room.

Sijiu chased after them and threw the rock at them with all his might. A dull sound came as the rock hit the tile floor and gouged a big hole in it. Sijiu rushed to Shanbo's side. "Master Liang! Master Liang!" He cried out, shaking him slightly.

Shanbo's face was full of blood. Somewhere from his head, a stream of blood was gushing down his face. Shanbo could hear Sijiu calling him, but was unable to move, his body aching, his mind unclear.

"Sijiu, get ... get out of ... here ... be ... before they come back to hurt you," he groaned. "Leave me behind. They ...

they cannot do ... do much more harm to ... to me." His voice was almost inaudible.

"No, Master Liang, I am taking you home with me." Sijiu lifted Shanbo up, threw him over his back and carried Shanbo out on his shoulders. Shanbo was too weak to protest. All he could say was "no ... no ... no."

Bending under Shanbo's weight, Sijiu walked out of the room a little unsteadily. Wencai Ma's men were standing outside, eyeing Sijiu with clubs in their hands.

"If you feel like dying today, I dare you to fight me. If not, stay out of my way," Sijiu shouted as he made for the door.

The men looked at each other. Not one ventured to move forward.

Sijiu carried Shanbo through the garden and got out of the front gate. He quickly placed him onto Dark Red and jumped onto the horse. Holding Shanbo tightly in his hands, Sijiu spurred the horse to gallop away toward home.

CHAPTER 19

WHEN THE ALL sweating Dark Red showed up in front of Shanbo's house at dusk, Old Master Liang and Mrs. Liang ran out of the house to take a look. They were horrified to see the blood-stained Shanbo leaning against Sijiu lifelessly.

"What happened?" Old Master asked in a shaking voice, while Mrs. Liang burst into tears.

"We had a fight," Sijiu said vaguely, not knowing how much to tell them. He signaled them to help get Shanbo off the horse.

"With whom?" Mrs. Liang asked, weeping. "Shanbo has never fought with anybody. What would have made him fight?"

"I don't know what happened exactly, but I do know it had to do with Miss Yingtai Zhu." As Sijiu said this, they carried Shanbo into his room.

"He did not go to Yingtai's home and confront her father, did he?" Old Master Liang asked.

"No, we went to Wencai Ma's house."

"How dare Shanbo go to that place?" Mrs. Liang began to see the whole picture.

"What else could have happened?" She cried, her heart aching as she examined Shanbo's wounds.

Shanbo groaned and opened his eyes with difficulty.

"Tell me what you want?" Mrs. Liang asked anxiously.

"Wa ... water."

Sijiu flew out of the room to get some drinking water. Mrs. Liang went out and brought back a basin of lukewarm water, while Old Master Liang was watching Shanbo with quiet anguish.

Shanbo took a mouthful of water, and let Mrs. Liang's shaking hands wash his wounds. His eyes stared blankly at the ceiling. "Why can we not be together?" He asked that question with all his strength before he was seized by a violent cough. "Wencai Ma is an evil man. He is going to torture Yingtai."

"Shanbo, you don't seem to understand life even with all your education. Who do you think you are, trying to reason with Wencai Ma? He could kill you at any time!" Old Mr. Liang said.

"This is not fair. Wencai Ma can do anything just because he is rich and powerful," Shanbo cried out in agony.

"Life has never been fair, Shanbo," Old Mr. Liang forced out these words, only to regret that it was too cruel to say so at this time.

Shanbo was about to say something, but his throat felt itchy. As he lowered his head to make himself feel better, several mouthfuls of blood erupted from him.

"Master Liang, Master Liang!" Sijiu was at a terrified loss.

Mrs. Liang sobbed when she saw the blood on the floor. "Shanbo! Take it easy. Don't harm yourself! There is still a chance for you and Yingtai as long as you stay well."

She ran out of the room and dragged in the big bag that Sijiu had brought back the day before. "Look, Shanbo, all these are from Yingtai. She wants you to get well."

Shanbo fell back to bed in exhaustion. His lips moved, but no words came out.

Mrs. Liang continued, "Shanbo, please hang on. We all depend on you to live. What is there in this world for me to look forward to if you are not here?"

Sijiu brought in some hot water and fed Shanbo a few mouthfuls.

Shanbo breathed noisily with difficulty. "I want to…to live for…for all of you. But I don't seem to have…have control over, my body," he fainted.

When Shanbo woke up, a doctor was working on him. Old Master Liang was sitting by his bedside with Yingtai's letter in his hand.

The doctor prescribed some medicine. Before leaving, he asked to talk to Old Master Liang in private.

"Your son has to want to live. Otherwise, there is no way he will recover."

Old Master Liang went to Shanbo's room with a forced smile. "Shanbo, Yingtai's letter is in fact very positive about your future. It will only take a little more time."

Shanbo shook his head. "Father, you don't know the whole story. Yingtai was just trying to give me a reason to live on. She herself has given up hope," he paused, unwilling to make his father feel bad, "unless, unless we die."

"You don't need to die; neither of you should die. You will make a very good couple. You just have to be patient."

Shanbo lay gasping for a while before he could go on. "Father, you are well read and you know how things are.

Yingtai is engaged to the son of the most powerful person in the region." His voice gradually went lower and slower. "Do you think that family is going to stand by if she rejects the marriage?"

"But Yingtai is an extraordinary woman. She has done the most incredible things for herself." Old Master tried to sound optimistic.

"That was something within her control. She just had to deal with her parents for that. But now her father is against her." Shanbo began to cough incessantly after these words. Fortunately, there was no blood this time.

Mrs. Liang, who had been sitting on the other end of the bed, weeping and praying, came to his side, to massage his temples.

Shanbo closed his eyes to collect enough energy before he could go on.

"The world believes that women are not entitled to participate in the decision of whom they marry, let alone whom they will not marry."

"I know," said Old Master Liang, "Yingtai is too good and thinks too far ahead for this world."

Shanbo opened his eyes in surprised but delighted agreement.

"That is why I went out of my way to defy Wencai Ma. I cannot let her go. Yingtai had been the only fighter till today. I am glad that I did my share of the fight."

Shanbo's spirit was up as he thought of his encounter with Wencai Ma. He was glad that he had endured humiliation for Yingtai, and that he had spit right into Wencai Ma's face. Somehow, he thought Yingtai was watching him and was proud of him.

"But that didn't change anything. Instead, you hurt yourself," Old Master Liang said.

"I know, but the most important thing is I have told Wencai Ma that he was not as powerful and as desirable as he thought he was, that I was not afraid of him, and that Yingtai did not care about his status."

"So what? You still cannot stop him from marrying Yingtai," Old Master Liang pointed out.

"But I know I can definitely be with her if we go to another world," Shanbo said with a glow of expectation in his face.

Old Master Liang was visibly distressed at hearing this. "Shanbo, your thinking is too wild. You must allow yourself some hope. And you cannot do that if you don't eat and sleep enough."

"Yes," Mrs. Liang broke in, "get some sleep now. I will cook you something nice to eat when you wake up."

Shanbo did not respond. His mind was drifting away. In a half awake state, he saw a large flower bed. He knew that Yingtai was somewhere nearby, but everything became cloudy when he tried to focus. He told himself to relax, and he followed a path that led him into the flowers. Then he heard his name being called. It was Yingtai! He turned round, and saw Yingtai in man's clothes, clothes she wore the first day they met.

He was rapturous. He repressed the urge of running toward her for fear that she would disappear. "Why are you in man's clothes?" he asked, pretending to be innocent. Yingtai laughed and began to walk toward him.

"You know I cannot walk on the road alone if I am a woman," she said.

"Oh, I forgot." Shanbo remembered all the trouble they had in order to fight against Yingtai's marriage to another man. "How did you get out of the house?" he asked in open admiration.

"That is a long story." Yingtai was getting nearer. All of a sudden, she dissolved into a cloudy blur.

"Yingtai, Yingtai! Don't leave me!" Shanbo cried despairingly.

Instantly, Yingtai was coming right in front of him again, wearing woman's clothes. "Here I am!" she said, looking like a triumphant little girl.

Shanbo was so carried away with exultation that he pulled her toward him. Yingtai threw her arms around him. It was the first time they hugged. It was the first time they were so intimate as a man and woman. Shanbo felt the waves of passion course through his body. "Oh, Yingtai, Yingtai!" he murmured in intoxicating happiness, smelling her, caressing her hair with his face.

Yingtai was blushing like a red flower. She wriggled a little in his arms, and raised her head to look at him. "I just came to tell you that I am yours. No one can take me away from you."

"You are safe now. I am not going to let you go even one step away from me," Shanbo said. He was going to say something else, but Yingtai had vanished without any warning. Shanbo was wild with the instant loss. "Yingtai, Yingtai!" He went all out calling her name, his hands waving in the air frenziedly.

He grabbed something in the middle of the air.

"Shanbo, Shanbo, wake up. You are hurting me!"

Shanbo opened his eyes, and found himself gripping his mother's hands. He was extremely thirsty, his lips cracking.

"My, you are running a high fever!" exclaimed Mrs. Liang. She called Old Master Liang into the room. They decided to send for the doctor again.

"Don't bother. It is no use." Shanbo stopped them feebly. "I am hungry and very thirsty."

Mrs. Liang brought in some porridge. "It has been boiling for a few minutes. It should be good for you. You must eat it hot. You will be better if you can sleep and sweat the fever out."

When Shanbo was half way through the porridge, Sijiu burst into the room in ecstasy. "Shun Wang is here. Yingtai has sent him!"

Shun Wang came into the room and saluted to everyone. He took a good look at Shanbo. "Miss Zhu sent me here to see you on her behalf. She also sent you some food and fruits."

"Thank you, Shun Wang."

"She knitted you a scarf. Here it is."

Shanbo accepted it quietly. "I am too weak to write today. Please tell her that I appreciate everything she has done for me and that I will see her again soon, somehow."

When Sijiu saw Shun Wang out, he briefed him of what had happened between Shanbo and Wencai Ma, and asked him to tell Yingtai about that.

After Shun Wang left, Shanbo asked Sijiu to put the scarf round his neck. It felt warm and soft, as warm and soft as Yingtai's hands. It was so sensual to be engulfed in the warmth created by her. He remembered something and sat up with a start. "Where is her hair?"

Mrs. Liang put her hand under his pillow and took the hair out. "You put it there before you fell asleep last night."

Shanbo took the hair. He ran his fingers over it. It felt soft and smooth like silk. It was like touching Yingtai. He dropped back onto bed and put the hair over his face. He asked his mother to make sure that the butterfly cloth was on his stomach. Then he held the two jade butterflies in his hands. After that, he called Sijiu to find the butterfly paper weight, the pomegranate pen container and the bronze mandarin ducks. He asked Sijiu to put them all by his pillow.

Shanbo gave a sigh of relief when this was done. He was now surrounded by Yingtai, and he felt very settled and warm. Mrs. Liang did not understand what these items meant to her son and was anxiety-ridden, thinking that her son was losing his mind. Sijiu whispered to her that they were all gifts from Yingtai.

Deeply touched and sincerely sorry for the lovers, Mrs. Liang could not contain herself. She had to go outside to collect herself. Sijiu followed her out.

Catching both Old Master Liang and Mrs. Liang in the sitting room, Sijiu said, "I was thinking that we must do something for them."

Old Master Liang looked up in surprise, wondering what he could have in mind.

"It may sound stupid, but I think this is worth a try." Sijiu took a deep breath and began.

"We should write to Taishou Ma, explaining to him that Miss Zhu and Master Liang had three years of friendship at school while Master Liang had no idea that Miss Zhu was a woman. When he found out the fact after Miss Zhu came home, they secretly made a commitment to each other. And that was before the Ma family made their proposal. Master

Zhu agreed to their proposal because he did not know the story at the time. We should also tell him what Wencai Ma did to Master Liang. Since Miss Zhu has said that she will not marry anyone except Master Liang, there is no point for the Ma family to prepare for the wedding. After reading our letter, Taishou Ma may think it disgraceful to force this unwanted marriage upon Miss Zhu and cancel the wedding."

Sijiu's face turned red. He had never spoken this much to the family.

Mrs. Liang thought Sijiu's idea made some sense, but Old Master Liang said it was a naive thought. "We may end up turning everything into a bigger mess. The best scenario would be that Taishou Ma ignores the letter, but I don't think he would appreciate that Master Zhu had kept from him the fact that Yingtai had been away from home for three years. It could be even worse than that. He could have us all arrested for defamation regardless of the facts. He could even prosecute the Zhu family for fraud and breach of engagement."

"You don't think he would simply give up Yingtai and let her have a future with Shanbo?" asked Mrs. Liang.

"Not unless he is out of his mind. I have never seen people like them showing a kind side," Old Master Liang said in distress.

"So all we can do is sit here and hope for the best?" Sijiu asked sorrowfully.

Old Master Liang did not answer. After a while, he told Sijiu to go and find another doctor.

Shanbo felt so good encircled by the things that had been so dear to Yingtai. His body became lighter and lighter until he could take to the air. Half floating and half drifting, he landed in Yingtai's garden. No one was in sight. He went to the bottom of the staircase leading to Yingtai's study and called her. There was some commotion in the room before Yingtai flew downstairs.

Yingtai came with a gust of wind, but she was not in human form. The gust of wind swept him up and he assumed the same form as Yingtai.

"What are we?" Shanbo asked.

"I am not sure, but I am hoping that we have turned into butterflies." Yingtai's words flew to him.

"Where are we going?"

"Anywhere we like. We are free now!"

"Are you sure? Can you promise me that you will not disappear again?"

"Yes, I can. We will definitely be together forever since we are no longer human beings."

"Is it that simple?" Shanbo was ecstatic.

"Yes, no one will be after us from now on. Let us fly!"

Shanbo followed her closely, afraid that she would be gone in no time. He fixed his eyes on her. Miraculously, she gradually changed in color, in form and finally turned into a butterfly, a pink one that was exactly like the one on the embroidery she had given him.

"Yingtai, wait for me. How can I turn myself into a butterfly?" Shanbo asked anxiously.

Butterfly Yingtai turned and cried out in exhilaration, "You are a butterfly already. Look at yourself!"

Shanbo looked at himself. Yes, he was a butterfly, a blue one just like the one Yingtai had created out of silk. He was unable to see the whole of himself, but he knew exactly how he looked.

"This is amazing! Everything worked out fine for us. Let us make this picture perfect. Let me fly a little ahead of you," Shanbo said.

"Then our wings can touch each other!" Yingtai added.

There they were, flying together in perfect harmony and absolute freedom.

Shanbo woke up in good spirits from the sweetest dream he had ever had. He had turned dismally thin and pitifully pale in the last few days. His body was aching from the blows he had received in Wencai Ma's study, but he had never felt better. In his mind he had gone to a better world with Yingtai. He knew he had to go for real this time.

He summoned his parents and Sijiu to his room.

"I am afraid my time is running out. Mother and Father, thank you for raising me all these years. I am so sorry that I will not live to take care of you in your old age. But I believe Sijiu will do that for me."

He turned to Sijiu.

"Sijiu, we have been like friends in many ways. You know my biggest concern is my parents. When I am gone, please take care of them for me. I am sure they will treat you like their son."

All three of them were in tears.

"Please don't go, my son. I don't want you to take care of me. I just want you to be healthy!" Mrs. Liang was so worn out by sadness that she could hardly make herself understood.

"Stay, Shanbo, please. You are giving us the worst experience any parent could ever have. If you go, there will be nothing left for us to live for!" Old Master Liang lost control of himself and sobbed miserably.

"Master Liang, don't say such depressing things. You are getting better. You ate and you talked for so long just now. Please be patient!" Sijiu was crying like a child.

"Please stop crying. I will be happy when I am gone. Yingtai will be with me. That is why I must go. You should be happy for me." Shanbo turned a little in bed. "Please do this for me: buy a small plot in the Huqiao county cemetery. I would like to be buried there."

He waited until his parents acknowledged that, and went on, "Sijiu, will you go and tell Yingtai after I have passed on? Tell her that I have tried my best to be with her. I think she will want to see me again in this world for the last time."

Sijiu nodded, unable to speak.

"Now will you help me lie in a better position? I want to look my best for Yingtai."

Sijiu did, his tears dropping onto Shanbo. Shanbo asked him to check to see that all the things from Yingtai were in the right places. Finally, he satisfied himself by moving Yingtai's hair from his face to his hair. He took a few pieces of the hair and started to chew them. Swallowing them down, he felt that he had Yingtai in him. Holding the jade butterflies in his hands, he said peacefully, "Now I am ready."

He looked up at the ceiling, and then beyond into the unknown. His breath was regular. His eyes showed eager expectation. After a while, his breathing slowed down, becoming weaker and weaker until there was no more air coming from him. However, his eyes were open, and the eager look of expectation in them made him look alive.

Old Master Liang, Mrs. Liang and Sijiu watched Shanbo die with amazement. Strangely enough, they stopped crying as they saw him departing, convinced that he was pain-free, and that he was setting off to a better world.

It was late evening. The three of them sat around Shanbo's body for a long time before Old Master Liang broke the silence.

"Sijiu, you had better leave for Yingtai's home tonight so that she can have time to decide whether she will come here or not."

CHAPTER 20

EVER SINCE YINGTAI heard the bad news about Shanbo's rapidly deteriorating health from Shun Wang, she had been waiting restlessly for more news to come. She had no idea how badly Shanbo had been injured by Wencai Ma. In fact, she could not imagine Shanbo dragging himself to travel that far to reason with Wencai Ma. She was shocked that he had done such a thing.

She had not quite decided what to do with herself as the set date for the wedding was drawing near. Her action would depend upon what happened to Shanbo. If he recovered, she would have to prepare her escape to the nunnery. The more she thought about it, the more she was convinced that it would be a good place for her.

If Shanbo could not make it, she would go after him. She did not know how yet, but she knew she would find a way.

It had been only half a day since Shun Wang came back, but it felt like years for Yingtai. She wished that she could turn herself into anything that could fly and fly out of the house to be at Shanbo's side. Yingtai became increasingly uneasy with each passing minute. After a sleepless night, she got up to ask Yinxin to pay a visit to the nunnery in the nearby mountain. She had convinced herself that Shanbo was well on his way to recovery, so she must run away from home before it was too late.

Yinxin tried to talk Yingtai into doing something less drastic, but Yingtai was not to be persuaded. Yinxin changed her mind instead and decided she would keep Yingtai's company in the nunnery.

Yinxin left after an early breakfast. She came back five minutes later followed by Sijiu.

Noticing there were tears in their eyes, Yingtai's heart sank. Her mind turned empty, and her eyes became blurring. A question was on the tip of her tongue, but she swallowed it.

"Miss Zhu!" Sijiu cried, kneeing down to the floor.

Yinxin helped him up. "Please, Sijiu, calm down and tell Miss Zhu what happened."

Sijiu wiped his tears and said, "Master Liang, he, he is gone!"

"Gone!" Though she had guessed it right, Yingtai was still unable to take it in.

"Shanbo is really gone?" She repeated it in a voice so low that she could barely hear herself.

"Before he died, he surrounded himself with all the things you had given him. He said he had tried his best to fight and he would be happier in another place where he could see you again."

Yingtai knew what that meant. She was happy that they had understood each other so well. But she missed the Shanbo that used to be so alive! Tears poured down her face as she realized that she could never see him alive in this world again.

"He died in great peace, and we were all with him. In fact, he was ready to die and he was in very good spirits."

Yingtai was somewhat relieved that Shanbo left in serenity, but was overwhelmed with grief over the loss of Shanbo. For a long time, she sat there sobbing, crying, and murmuring to herself.

Suddenly, Yingtai realized that Yinxin and Sijiu were still in her study.

"Did he leave any words?" she asked, dreamily.

"He mentioned some family issues. Yes, he said we should let you know when he was gone. You might want to see him for the last time."

"When did he pass away?"

"Last evening. We will not move him until you decide whether or not to go see him."

Yingtai jumped up. "I will leave right away. Yinxin, tell them to get the cart ready."

"You must ask Master Zhu for permission," Yinxin reminded her.

"I will go even if he does not give the permission."

"No one dares to prepare the cart for you if Master Zhu does not give the word."

"I guess you are correct. Sijiu, you wait for us downstairs. Yinxin, you come with me to my parents. I will kill myself right on the spot if they refuse me."

"Please," Yinxin said, "you can threaten them with that, but you must not actually do it!" Yinxin warned.

Gongyuan Zhu and Mrs. Zhu had just awoken and were surprised to see Yingtai and Yinxin so early.

"What is the matter?" Mrs. Zhu said, noticing the traces of tears on both of them.

"Sijiu came to inform me that Shanbo died last night."

"He is dead?" Gongyuan Zhu was partly shocked and partly relieved.

"We spent three years together and we were great friends. I have to go and say good-bye to him in person. I am here to ask permission to go. Please understand."

"You want to go and say good-bye to him?" Gongyuan Zhu and Mrs. Zhu asked simultaneously.

"Yes!"

"Are you mad? You are engaged to someone else! You are not supposed to have any male friends. You are not even supposed to walk out there!"

"Shanbo was my brother. I cannot let him go without paying my last respects!" Yingtai said adamantly.

"You cannot go!" Gongyuan Zhu insisted.

"I must go!" Yingtai took the scissors that were sitting in the window sill and pointed them to her throat. "Either I go or you watch me die right here."

Mrs. Zhu shook with fright. "Yingtai, put the scissors down! If you want to go, just go. There is no need for scissors."

Yingtai did not move. "Are you speaking for father or just for yourself?"

Gongyuan Zhu was humiliated, but he could not afford to save face by risking his daughter's life.

"I will allow you to go, but only under three conditions."

"What are they?"

"Number one, you must not wear mourning apparel. Number two, you must go with a group of people. And Number three, you must return immediately."

He cleared his throat unnecessarily to give some force to his words. "Your wedding is only days away."

"Yes, I can do all of this, as long as I can take the cart and Yinxin. You may send whomever you choose to accompany me."

Yingtai and Yinxin headed toward the door.

"Yinxin, please take good care of Yingtai," Mrs. Zhu said.

Yingtai took off all the accessories she was wearing and changed into monochromatic clothing. Yinxin prepared a package under Yingtai's instruction.

They then rushed into the cart where Sijiu and three other servants were waiting. The horses ran most of the way. A little over three hours later, they were close to Shanbo's house.

Yingtai stopped the cart, took out the package Yinxin had prepared for her and found a place to change into a white mourning dress. She fixed her hair into a bun that only married women wore, and was dressed and coifed like a widow.

A crowd of neighbors gathered outside the Liang house when the cart arrived. They were curious to see who the visitors were. They all knew that Shanbo was not a married man, and were astounded to see Yingtai wearing mourning clothes with her hair tied up in a matronly bun. Amazement quickly turned to admiration as they learned her story with Shanbo. They marveled at her beauty even in grief.

Sijiu directed Yingtai's gaze toward the sad-looking couple at the door and told her that they were Old Master Liang and Mrs. Liang. Yingtai went toward them and the couple came up to greet her.

"Thank you for coming all this way," Old Master Liang said.

"Thank you for letting me know," Yingtai said, holding Mrs. Liang by the hand.

Mrs. Liang was in tears. "Thank you for dressing like this for Shanbo. If he knew you were mourning him in this way, he would be extremely grateful."

Old Master Liang said, "This is not the place to talk. Let us go inside."

They went into the sitting room. Yingtai insisted on dropping a formal curtsy to Old Master Liang and Mrs. Liang. Then she inquired about the arrangements for Shanbo's funeral.

"The clothes and the coffin are all ready. We will dress him and lay him to rest after you have seen him."

"May I see him now?" Yingtai asked, fighting back her tears.

"Please come with me," Old Master Liang said.

Yingtai followed him to Shanbo's bedroom. Dozens of white candles were laid on the floor marking a path up to the bed where Shanbo lay.

Yingtai quickened her steps as soon as she saw Shanbo. She stopped short by the bed full of tears. She bent down to look at him quietly as if she were afraid of waking him up. Shanbo was in a vest that he used to wear indoors when he was at school. It showed his arms and shoulders, and Yingtai had once used to avoid looking at him dressed so sparsely out of modesty. But now she devoured every inch that she could lay her eyes on so that she could remember his form for ever.

Her eyes fell upon the gifts she had given him. They must have been all around him when he died. He must have been thinking of her to the very end. Yingtai could not bear to think that she was not there for him during his last moments. Had she come to see him when he summoned her, he might not have died. She wished she had been with him when he challenged Wencai Ma.

Yingtai did not cry. She was too sad to cry. The pain simply went deep inside. It penetrated her body and mind. As she twisted with torment, she lost consciousness.

Mrs. Liang and Yinxin were there in time to stop her from hitting the floor.

Mrs. Liang cried out, "Shanbo, are your eyes still open? Are you expecting Yingtai? She is here. Can't you see her? Do something. Show her that you know she is here!"

Yingtai opened her eyes at this. She bent close to Shanbo, "Shanbo, why are your eyes still open?"

"I think he wants to see you," Old Master Liang suggested.

Yingtai knelt down by Shanbo, and whispered into his ears, "Please close your eyes if I speak correctly. Are you worried that no one will take care of your parents? Your uncles and aunts are all here and Sijiu is here too. Don't worry. They will take care of your parents."

Shanbo lay motionless.

"Do you regret quitting school?"

Shanbo was stone-still.

"Are you frustrated because you don't know what will happen to me?"

Yingtai was staring deeply into Shanbo's eyes as she questioned him, massaging his upper eyelids softly. At the third question, Shanbo's eyes seemed to flicker. Yingtai's heart ached.

"The only thing that will happen to me is that I will soon join you in the grave. Your tombstone will have one next to it bearing my name."

She raised her voice so that those in the room could hear her.

"We could not be husband and wife during our life time, but I am going to make sure that we will be together after death."

She continued to massage Shanbo's eyelids. When she finished this declaration, Shanbo's eyes closed completely. Everyone in the room was mystified and shed tears of sadness and joy at their magical communication.

"Shanbo said he wanted to look good for you. He arranged himself in this tableau," Old Master Liang said. "I think he is holding the jade butterflies in his hands."

Shanbo's hands were clenched into fists. Yingtai pried one of them gently open and took the butterfly nestled in his palm.

"You keep the other one, Shanbo. They will be a couple as soon as we meet again." She gazed at the butterfly needlework she had made for him. It was covering the upper part of Shanbo's body, across his chest. It was difficult for her to see the two butterflies enjoy such freedom while she and Shanbo were divided by two different worlds. Yingtai hesitated, then secured the cloth in her hands.

"I am taking it because I need it more than you do now. I need to look at it often to convince myself that we are still together."

Yingtai stood up. "I think Shanbo is ready to go," she said, turning very pale.

"Yingtai, you must take a rest," said Mrs. Liang.

Yingtai followed her mechanically to the adjacent room, but she refused to lie down, "I simply cannot sleep now."

Yinxin followed them into the room. "Miss, you must be exhausted. Lying down cannot hurt. You don't have to sleep, just rest. Master Liang would never want to see you so tired."

This made sense to Yingtai. All at once, she felt very weak from fatigue. She let Yinxin lay her down.

"Yinxin, you must be tired and hungry yourself. Please go and tell Sijiu to find you something to eat and then prepare a room for you to rest in as well," Mrs. Liang said with concern.

Yinxin looked at Yingtai and said, "I think I will follow your advice. Neither of us can afford to be sick right now."

"She is a very nice girl," Mrs. Liang commented after Yinxin had left.

"Yes, she has been a good friend and great help to me," Yingtai said. "In fact, I have long been convinced that Sijiu and Yinxin would make a good match. Some day, I will no longer be here to watch over Yinxin. If she and Sijiu were to marry, they could take very good care of you and Old Master Liang. I trust that you would treat her like your daughter."

"Of course we would! But what do you mean that you will not be here to take care of her some day?"

"Well, that is my concern. Anyway, she cannot be with me all her life. She will have to marry and leave me someday."

Mrs. Liang decided it would not be a good idea to pursue the subject any further. She dropped the topic to talk about Shanbo. "We have purchased a burial plot in the Huqiao county cemetery, according to Shanbo's wishes."

This was of great concern to Yingtai. "That is wonderful. Shanbo and I once talked about that."

"You did?"

"Yes, we agreed that we would rest together in the same grave after death."

Mrs. Liang was amazed.

"Will you please make sure that when they prepare Shanbo's tombstone, you purchase another one and have my name engraved upon it? Then I would like you to place it next to Shanbo's at the cemetery," Yingtai said, ignoring Mrs. Liang's shocked look.

"What a bizarre request! But you are still living! Why on earth would you want me to have a tombstone prepared for you?" exclaimed Mrs. Liang.

"Because that's my wish. If the idea is too wild for you, or if you cannot bring yourself to place my tombstone next to Shanbo's, I can ask you to just bury mine beneath the earth, next to his grave."

Mrs. Liang did not know what to say.

"Please, do me this favor. I asked because Shanbo and I have talked about this. I have no way of knowing whether this request will be honored by my parents after my death, so I need to make the arrangement with you. I am simply being practical. Shanbo and I wish to be buried together after death. But this does not necessarily mean I am about to die in the immediate future!"

Mrs. Liang was still speechless.

"Please! I cannot leave unless you promise me that you will do this for me and Shanbo," Yingtai said persistently.

"All right, I promise."

A servant came in to report that Shanbo was ready to be placed into the coffin and taken to the Huqiao county cemetery for burial.

Mrs. Liang and Yingtai went into Shanbo's bedroom to see him for the last time before they took him away for the funeral rites. Shanbo was wrapped in a burial shroud, looking very peaceful.

It dawned upon Yingtai that these were her last moments with Shanbo. She threw herself onto his bed and cried out. "Shanbo! Oh my sweet Shanbo!" She clasped his hands into hers and drew them up to her face.

Yinxin and Sijiu came and gently pried her off of Shanbo. Yingtai did not resist. She simply fainted into their arms.

When she came to, Yingtai found Yinxin and Mrs. Liang weeping quietly by her side.

"They have taken him away," said Mrs. Liang.

"If you are feeling up to it, Miss, we should be leaving soon. It will not do you any good to stay here any longer," Yinxin suggested gently.

Yingtai agreed. Before leaving, she wanted to participate in the memorial ritual that was about to be conducted in the sitting room. She knelt down before the offerings and candles that surrounded Shanbo's bier.

"Shanbo, I have to leave you now. Please find a way to visit me. I don't know of your world, but you know mine and you know where you can find me," she whispered.

Old Master Liang and Mrs. Liang urged Yingtai to go, "You should go now. Your parents will be worried."

Yingtai curtsied to them. "Goodbye. Please take good care of yourselves. If there is any news, please send Sijiu to visit me."

"It was so kind and so brave of you to come. We will always be indebted to you. Shanbo was very lucky to have known you and loved you." Old Master Liang and Mrs. Liang felt that they could not thank Yingtai enough.

CHAPTER 21

YINGTAI STOPPED THE cart when they were near home and changed into her regular clothing. She did not say a word during the entire return trip. They got home after midnight. Gongyuan Zhu and Mrs. Zhu were still awake. They called for Yingtai and asked her questions. Yingtai answered them tersely. Her parents let her go without further queries knowing that she had had a rather traumatic evening.

The next day, Yingtai spent the whole day in her room. Gongyuan Zhu and Mrs. Zhu were beginning to get nervous because her wedding was to take place in just five days, but they decided to leave her alone for the next two days to get over Shanbo's death. Gongyuan Zhu was confident that since Shanbo was gone, Yingtai had no reason to reject Wencai Ma.

Yingtai slid deeper into a fantasy world. She stared at the willows outside her window until she could see Shanbo emerging from the leaves. Yingtai was not surprised to see Shanbo at all.

"I knew you would find a way back to see me," she said.

"I did not have to find a way back." Shanbo laughed as he jumped nimbly onto the window sill. "I never actually died. I staged my death in order to find enough time to build us a house hidden deep in the mountains."

Yingtai was thrilled. "How come you did not even give me a clue? I had the most torturous moments saying goodbye to you."

"Only so you would be deliriously happy when you found out the truth!" Shanbo said more playfully than he had ever been.

"Should we go now? Or should we wait until night falls so we can leave under the cover of darkness?"

"We can go now. But first we have to become invisible so that we can go wherever and do whatever we want without being seen."

"How?"

"I will show you," Shanbo said and disappeared in a flash.

Yingtai waited for herself to lose her physical existence, but nothing happened. She was getting fretful when she heard Yinxin's voice.

"Miss, Sijiu is here."

Yingtai was glad to be awakened from a frustrating dream.

Sijiu had come straight from Huqiao county after Shanbo's burial.

"Old Master Liang wanted you to know that everything for the funeral was taken care of. It is now over."

"Did Mrs. Liang send a message?"

"Yes, she mentioned your tombstone. She has had it buried right below the surface under Master Liang's as you requested."

"Tell me exactly where the grave is."

Sijiu said it was in Nine Dragon Cemetery, located right beside the Yong River.

"From the cemetery, you can hear people talking in the boats as they pass. It is a beautiful final resting place for Master Liang," Sijiu choked.

The next day, Mrs. Zhu came in to see Yingtai, who was staring blankly out of the window.

Yingtai greeted her but showed no interest in having a conversation.

"I know you are still grieving for Shanbo. But you have done all you could for him. He and his parents must be happy and grateful for that. Now you have to move on with your life," said Mrs. Zhu.

"I think I am moving on all right."

"As you know, the Ma family will be coming for you shortly for the wedding." Mrs. Zhu embarked on the sensitive topic.

"I don't know of any Ma family and I am not going to any wedding. Did I not make myself clear in our previous talks?" Yingtai snapped impatiently.

"Yingtai, this is going to be the most important day of your life. You must begin to get serious about it."

"I am quite serious about it. I am going to say this just one more time: I will not be available."

"They could use force to get you to the altar," Mrs. Zhu warned.

"No one can force me to do anything. Not even the emperor himself! The only place they can force me to go is my grave. And then I would be with Shanbo forever."

"You don't know what you are talking about ..." Mrs. Zhu became very upset. She got up to leave. "Your father is going to have a talk with you tomorrow. You must be careful with what you say and you must show him proper respect."

Yingtai gave her mother an I-don't-care look, smirking sarcastically.

That same evening, Mrs. Zhu told Gongyuan Zhu that Yingtai was still very hostile to the idea of marrying Wencai Ma. He was so irritated that he wanted to teach Yingtai a lesson immediately. Mrs. Zhu suggested that he should change his approach. Instead of impatience, he should show willingness to negotiate.

"You know your daughter. She never compromises under pressure. But if you are nice about it, she may not be too rebellious," Mrs. Zhu suggested.

The next day, Yingtai was summoned to her father.

"Congratulations!" Gongyuan Zhu smiled from ear to ear as he said this.

"For what?" Yingtai asked coldly.

"On your upcoming wedding!" Gongyuan Zhu tried to sound enthusiastic to cover his frustration.

"I cannot have a wedding! I have already married myself to Shanbo."

"That is absurd!" The words came out before Gongyuan Zhu could stop himself. He stood up and walked a bit to calm himself.

Sitting back in his seat, he said, "How can you marry yourself?"

"How can you marry me off to a person without consulting me? Does that make any more sense than for me to marry myself to someone?"

"All right, Yingtai. For the sake of argument, let us say that you could marry yourself." Gongyuan Zhu softened his tone as he struggled to keep his rage down. "But Shanbo is now dead, and there is nothing substantial between you two any longer. You are completely free. You can certainly marry another person."

"No, I have to keep my chastity for Shanbo. That is the duty of a widow. This is what Confucius said."

Gongyuan Zhu was tongue-tied for a minute. "You are getting even more absurd. The truth is that Shanbo was never your husband. He can claim no rights over you whatsoever."

"Then Wencai Ma has no right to marry me either. Why are you making me marry him? Is it because he is rich and his father has influence? You, my father, are acting no better than a slave trader. You quiver with fear and humble yourself in front of the Ma family simply because they are wealthy and powerful. You think that this marriage arrangement between Wencai Ma and me will give you access to their prestige and wealth. You are selling your only daughter to that family simply to satisfy your vanity and to increase your social standing in the community."

Gongyuan Zhu blew up. "You are completely out of your mind. How dare you say this to me?" He gave the desk a hard punch.

Mrs. Zhu was very upset too. "Yingtai, you know your father and I can survive financially quite well without looking to anyone for the rest of our lives. And our social standing has always been of the highest order. Why would we use you in such a way? We need neither money nor influence from the Ma family. It truly wounds us to hear you speak this way of your father. You must apologize."

"You are right. I am angry, and I am just lashing out without much thinking. That was a very hurtful thing to say and for that I can apologize. I know that you just want me to have a good future. But I know I can never have a happy life without Shanbo."

"I think that is enough conversation for today. Let us all calm down a bit. Perhaps we will be able to better understand each other tomorrow," Mrs. Zhu concluded.

Yingtai gave her father an angry look. She knew that nothing would be resolved from this talk.

"All right, I am leaving. But there is no way I will ever change my mind. Never."

Yingtai went back to her room and told Yinxin what had happened.

"What are you going to do?" Yinxin looked very worried.

"I was prepared to see my father that way. Don't fret. I know how to handle it," Yingtai said with strange serenity.

Yinxin was puzzled. Yingtai had always let her know what was on her mind, but not this time.

"But Master and Mrs. Zhu will never let you have any peace until you agree to this marriage," Yinxin said, trying to find out what solution Yingtai had to her problem.

"I know," Yingtai said with confidence. "When it gets too bad, I shall have to resort to the extreme. Now please keep quiet. I will not tell you anything more than this."

The next morning, Mrs. Zhu came to Yingtai's study. Having heard her footsteps, Yingtai picked up a book pretending to read. She did not move her eyes off the book until her mother called her twice.

"Good morning, mother," Yingtai said, withholding any emotion.

"I want to talk to you," Mrs. Zhu sat down.

"I know what is about. You will be repeating what father said yesterday and I will give you the same response," Yingtai said with indifference, and turned her eyes back to the book.

"Please put down the book so we can have a real talk."

"About what?" Yingtai looked at her mother with disinterest, closing the book.

"You said you would not marry Wencai Ma. If that is the case, what are you going to do with yourself at home?"

"I will take care of you and father."

"But we will die some day."

"By that time I will be pretty old too. I will spend all my time reading and keeping you company."

"Don't speak such nonsense! As a woman, you need to have a husband, a family, a son ..."

"Enough. Please stop." Yingtai picked up the book again.

Mrs. Zhu got up quietly, shaking her head.

"All right. I will leave this up to your father."

Gongyuan Zhu could tell from his wife's long face that Yingtai had not changed her mind.

"What am I to do? She has been threatening to kill herself rather than marry Wencai Ma. We cannot afford to offend the Ma family, but we cannot see Yingtai take her own life either." He paced the room back and forth with his hands clasped behind his back.

"Listen," he turned to his wife, "the reason why Yingtai refuses to get married is Shanbo Liang. If we go and ask her what she wants to do about it before she could accept this marriage, she may come up with some conditions. If we let her have her way at first, perhaps we could have our way afterwards."

When Mrs. Zhu asked Yingtai what could make her accept the marriage, Yingtai looked out of the window for a long while, "I don't think there is a way."

Mrs. Zhu became very upset. "Yingtai, it made sense to me that you refused to marry Wencai Ma when Shanbo was alive. But he is gone, and you cannot go on like this forever. Please be reasonable as you are worrying us to death."

For a long while Yingtai looked at her mother sorrowfully. She decided that it was time to call her parents' bluff.

"I will do what you want me to if you allow me to go and visit Shanbo's graveyard on the way to the Ma family."

Mrs. Zhu's face lit up. "Did I hear you correct? You will marry Wencai Ma if we allow you to visit Shanbo's grave on your way to the wedding?"

"Yes. That means we will have to detour to Huqiao county where Shanbo rests."

Mrs. Zhu almost danced back to her husband's study. "Yingtai said yes!"

Gongyuan Zhu jumped up from his chair. "Excellent! What does she want in return?"

"She said she must visit Shanbo's grave on her way to the Ma family. This means that we will have to tell the Ma family the entire story. I cannot imagine what kind of shock it will be for Taishou Ma. Do you think he can handle the truth?"

"We don't have a choice. Taishou Ma may simply accept it in order to save face. If he makes a fuss, everyone will know that it was he who proposed to us without fully investigating Yingtai's background."

"It sounds this is the only way to make the marriage happen," Mrs. Zhu said, feeling very disturbed.

"I cannot possibly go and tell Taishou Ma myself," Gongyuan Zhu said in a troubled voice.

"You don't have to. Let Matchmaker Qiu do it. She will do it for the right price. You know, if there is no marriage, she will not receive payment anyway. Moreover, the Ma family might punish her for making such a bad deal for them. She will just have to convince the family to go ahead with the wedding no matter what."

They sent for Matchmaker Qiu immediately. She frowned upon hearing the story. "What am I going to do about this? Such a story is unprecedented. I don't see any chance of convincing the Ma family to continue with the wedding at all, let alone agree to this pre-condition!"

Gongyuan Zhu warned her that she would not get paid by the Ma family if the marriage fell through. In addition, she would bear the added stigma of having brokered the family a bad deal. Though very frustrated, Matchmaker Qiu agreed to speak with Wencai Ma for she believed that he truly admired and desired Yingtai.

"I don't care who you talk to or how you do it as long as you make the whole thing work," said Gongyuan Zhu.

There were only two days before the wedding. Matchmaker Qiu set off to the Ma family right away. She had a difficult conversation with Wencai Ma.

"Master Ma, I don't know how to say this, but there is something that I must tell you about Miss Yingtai Zhu." Matchmaker Qiu began in a small voice.

"I think I can guess what it is," Wencai Ma said with a hardened smile.

"I don't think you possibly could, Master Ma," Matchmaker Qiu said. "I myself only just found out about it. Did you know about ... about her ... having left home and gone to school?" she asked timidly.

"And much more," Wencai Ma said, his face turning dark.

"If you know that, may I assume that you also know about the man she met there?" Matchmaker Qiu was both relieved and nervous.

"Oh, yes," Wencai said lightheartedly, but Matchmaker Qiu could tell that he was actually quite agitated.

"And you know that he has died?" She kept on checking how informed he was.

"He has?" Now it was Wencai Ma's turn to be surprised. Instantly, a smile came to his face. "Poor thing!" He commented in a cheerful voice, showing no attempt to hide his pleasure.

Matchmaker Qiu saw her chance. "As far as I can see, it would be a good idea for you to act generously in this case. You see, if you decide to cancel the marriage, it would be your loss. You could scarcely find a woman that is as remotely talented or as beautiful as Miss Zhu. You could lose face as well. You know, people would laugh at you if they knew the story. They would think that your father made a rather stupid proposal."

Seeing that Wencai Ma was all ears, she added, "Yingtai Zhu has come to her senses. She wants to get married, but she has one request."

"What is it?" Wencai Ma asked curiously.

"Before she comes to your house for the wedding, she wants to make a stop at the cemetery in Huqiao county in order to pay Shanbo Liang's grave a visit. She said they had been friends and she wants to say good-bye to him."

"What a bitch!" Wencai Ma cursed between his teeth. "She will pay for this!"

"This is true! You will have plenty of time to punish her for this after the wedding. You will be her master as soon as she becomes your wife," Matchmaker Qiu continued. "Besides, Shanbo Liang is dead, and she cannot pine away for him forever. She has already promised that this would be her only visit."

For some time, Wencai Ma did not say anything.

"Please don't be offended by my telling you this: If you reject Yingtai Zhu, you will regret it for the rest of your life. I could never find another woman for you as good as she is. If you try to save a little, you lose a lot."

Wencai Ma was very uncomfortable with this twist to the impending marriage. He felt challenged, but realized that Matchmaker Qiu was actually making sense.

"Well, even if I can take this, my father will not," he said.

Matchmaker Qiu thought this a good sign. "You don't have to tell him the story, do you? After all, he will not be going to the Zhus to pick up Yingtai Zhu. No one dare tell him what happens along the way if you forbid them to."

Finally, Wencai Ma gave in. "But I must insist that you tell her that she may not wear mourning clothes. She must wear the traditional bridal red on her way here."

Matchmaker Qiu rejoiced over this, promising to convey this information on to the Zhu family. They then decided that the Ma family would use the waterway, instead of the road, to come and pick up Yingtai because that would make the detour to Huqiao county a lot easier.

Matchmaker Qiu rushed to tell Gongyuan Zhu and Mrs. Zhu to get ready for the wedding. The entire household was instantly filled with excitement. Under Mrs. Zhu's instruction, everybody set to making preparations.

Yingtai was exceptionally calm about the whole affair. She did not do anything except asking Yinxin to make sure that the butterfly embroidery was by her bed so that she could wear it as a scarf on the special occasion.

"I am glad you are getting married," Yinxin said while packing, waiting to see Yingtai's reaction.

Yingtai smiled. "What you are trying to say is that you cannot believe that I am actually going to marry Wencai Ma."

Yinxin could not bring herself to comment. She avoided Yingtai's eyes and played with a corner of her clothes.

"I know what I am doing. Now you had better make a decision for yourself. What are you going to do when I get married?"

Yinxin said without thinking, "I will go wherever you go."

"I know. But I want you to tell me what you want for your future."

Yinxin looked out of the window without a word.

"Let me say it for you. You would like to marry Sijiu."

Yinxin gave a sweet smile.

"I will make sure that this happens for you. When the time comes, someone will find a go-between for you even if I am not here to do it for you myself. But for now, you are to accompany me. You will soon understand why I am doing all this."

The next afternoon, two boats came for Yingtai. The Ma family had sent over fifty people for the occasion. Thirty-two men played trumpets along the way while a few men hoisted colorful banners. Eight strong men carried a luxurious sedan for the bride to ride in. All were dressed in red silk clothing, with golden embroidery throughout the fabric.

Yingtai sat in her room with a disgusted look as the sound of the music came near. Yinxin and Mrs. Zhu had been helping her to put on her wedding clothes. Yingtai insisted on wearing very light make-up. She also insisted on wearing white mourning clothes beneath her favorite pink shirt.

Mrs. Zhu said pleadingly, "Yingtai, this is your wedding! You should be happy or at least appear to be happy. Please put on the red wedding dress."

"Mother, I don't feel happy. Why should I pretend to be happy for others? For me, the most important thing is that I am mourning for Shanbo. You know, the trip will last one and a half days. I will have plenty of time to dress up before I get to the final destination. I will spend all my time making myself beautiful after paying my respects to Shanbo," she promised.

"I see your point, but please do this for your father and me. Please wear the red dress when the sedan is here. You can take it off when you are in the boat."

At this, Yingtai's eyes suddenly filled with tears. She looked at her mother sorrowfully, then said slowly, "Yes, Mother, I will do this for you, if you feel it is that important. I am sorry I have been keeping you so worried and unhappy. As soon as I am gone from here, your troubles will be over."

"Don't be so silly, Yingtai," Mrs. Zhu began to feel sad too. "You have been a wonderful daughter. I am sorry for all that has happened. I only hope that you will find much happiness in your marriage. You know we are going to miss you very much."

For a time, Yingtai and Mrs. Zhu wept together until Yinxin reminded them that the team from the Ma family was there. A minute later, a servant was sent by Gongyuan Zhu to urge Yingtai out.

Mrs. Zhu wiped the tears from Yingtai's face. "This should be a happy day for you." She then turned to Yinxin. "Prepare Yingtai's facial makeup."

When Yingtai stepped out of her room into the sitting room, Gongyuan Zhu was waiting impatiently. He was clad in red and gold, matching the outfit that Mrs. Zhu was wearing. Matchmaker Qiu was all smiles, also dressed in red. She was most animated and appeared the happiest of all.

Outside the gate, the elaborately decorated sedan was laid on the ground. Eight men, four on each side, stood to await Yingtai.

Traditionally, the bride's parents don't go with the bride to the groom's family. But since the boat trip would take over a day and Yingtai would make a stop in Huqiao county, Gongyuan Zhu and Mrs. Zhu decided to accompany Yingtai as far as Huqiao county, to ensure that everything went as planned. They wanted to make sure that Yingtai would be safely off on her way to the Ma family.

The dock where the two boats were anchored was a quarter of a mile away from the Zhu house. Gongyuan Zhu ordered that Yingtai's dowry be placed into the boat with the people from the Ma family. Yingtai, seated in the sedan and led by thirty-eight trumpet blowers, boarded the other boat with Yinxin. Gongyuan Zhu and Mrs. Zhu climbed onto the same boat after them.

The boats were decorated with colorful fresh flowers and had red streamers strung along all of the windows. Yingtai's private cabin was located in the aft. The trip went smoothly the first day, though the boats had to move slowly and carefully along the meandering river. It was the peak of spring. Everything was bursting with new life. Yingtai was quiet throughout the day. She claimed motion sickness to prevent her parents from coming in and attempting to engage her in conversation.

Early next morning, they sailed up the Yong River which ran through Huqiao county. Yingtai became agitated and kept looking out of the cabin, trying to catch a glimpse of Nine Dragon Cemetery. Time and again, she sent Yingtai to the steersman to find out when they would arrive at their destination.

Suddenly, a wave crashed over the boat, followed by many more. The boatman lowered the sails, but that did not stop the boat from pitching to and fro wildly. There were a few other boats in sight. They too became victims of treacherous winds. She watched as many struggled helplessly in the river. The boat's lurching tossed her from one side of the cabin to the other. She could see the foam from the waves dashing against the rear of the boat. She could also see that they were dangerously close to shore. When she glimpsed out, houses were just visible behind trees that were blowing madly along the river's edge. Yingtai went to the boatman and asked where they were. It turned out to be Nine Dragon Cemetery in Huqiao county. "Please, we must make a stop here!" Yingtai shouted over the screaming winds.

"We have to. The river is getting too rough for the boats," said the boatman.

Yingtai became very much alive as the boat headed toward the bank.

Gongyuan Zhu looked at the river and thought to himself: what a strange coincidence. The river was so calm until we arrived at this place. He became a little worried, and asked the steersman how long these rough conditions would likely last.

"A rainstorm is coming, but I doubt it will last very long. We shall drop anchor here and wait it out."

Gongyuan Zhu felt relieved at this. The wind was blowing so hard that one could hardly stand up straight. The boatman managed to steer into a cove and drop anchor.

Yingtai went to her parents' cabin. "Father, Mother, we are at Nine Dragon Cemetery. I am going to go up there to see Shanbo. How many people do you want me to take along?"

"Just take Yinxin with you. But I cannot interfere with people from the Ma family. They might send a few people to go with you." Gongyuan Zhu said.

"I don't care."

Mrs. Zhu had not said anything but kept her eyes on her daughter. Yingtai had dressed up: her hair held back in a bun like a married woman with jade hairpins glittering; her butterfly embroidery worn as a scarf; a pink silk shirt with patterns of peonies; a dark blue skirt and a pair of high-soled shoes with phoenix heads on the front. Her face was colored attractively with lipstick and rouge.

"You are dressed like this to mourn Shanbo?" Mrs. Zhu asked in disbelief.

"I have mourning clothes on underneath." Yingtai reminded her mother. "Besides, I wanted to make myself look pretty for Shanbo."

Gongyuan Zhu said, "Maybe you should wait until the rainstorm is over."

"No, I think it is a better idea to go before the rain gets here. I don't think it will rain for a while yet," Yingtai said.

"Father, Mother, I am leaving now." She moved hesitantly toward the boat side.

"Come back as soon as you can," said Mrs. Zhu.

Yingtai wanted to stay a little longer, but was afraid that her father would become suspicious.

"Take good care of yourselves," she turned away quickly.

The servants from the Ma family had lined up along the bank when Yingtai and Yinxin stepped off of the boat. The servants stood there quietly as the two walked toward a small forest. Five men followed them from a respectful distance.

Yingtai and Yinxin followed a path leading from the center of the forest into a grassy cemetery. They came upon a newly dug plot of land covered with fresh topsoil . A stone marker in front of it read:

Here Lies Shanbo Liang

Yingtai's whole body trembled. She ran and knelt in front of the grave.

"Shanbo, Shanbo, it is me, Yingtai. I have come to join you as I promised."

As she said this, a gust of wind blew by, whistling through the tree tops. The sky looked golden yellow. Yinxin stood a few steps away from Yingtai, waiting for her to finish her prayer.

Yingtai looked around the gravesite.

"Shanbo, we agreed that there would be two grave markers in front of the grave. I know mine was placed beneath yours. Would you please show it to me?" She held herself onto the gravestone bearing Shanbo's name and began to weep.

The golden yellow sky turned dark all at once. For a moment, one could scarcely see anything. Suddenly, lightening flashed and a deafening thunder exploded so loudly that Yinxin, who had never experienced such inclement weather in her life, trembled and buried her face in her hands.

The sky seemed to have been broken open by the thunder and torrential rain. At that moment, Shanbo's grave opened a crack. As if pushed up by someone, a headstone surged up from the grave and landed right next to Yingtai. It had "Yingtai Zhu" engraved upon it.

Incredibly, the driving rain did not seem to reach Yingtai at all. Her clothes remained bone dry and she stood motionless like a statue. When she saw the gravestone, she went wild with ecstasy.

"Please, Shanbo, open the door for me! Let me join you!" She cried at the top of her voice.

It was such a loud cry that it made the ground shake. Shanbo's grave shook more violently. With an uproarious sound from within, Shanbo's grave was ripped wide open. Brightly colored light rays were emanating from the split earth.

"Shanbo, I am coming!" With these final words, Yingtai jumped up and flew down into the grave. As soon as she got inside, the grave closed in upon itself.

Yinxin was standing behind Yingtai as it all happened. She felt the shaking of the earth and saw Shanbo's grave open. She was awestruck and frozen in place. When Yingtai ran toward the grave, Yinxin was just coming back to her senses. She screamed and stretched out both hands to grab Yingtai. But Yingtai was so fast that all Yinxin managed to get was two pieces of fabric from Yingtai's pink shirt and blue skirt. Yinxin fell backwards as she fought to hold onto Yingtai. She heard the sound of the fabric ripping, and by the time she managed to look up, the grave was already closed. Shanbo's grave resumed its original shape and there was a new one by its side which had Yingtai's name on it.

"Miss!" Yinxin cried out hysterically, her arms stretching out, her hands open. The small pieces of pink and blue cloth escaped from her hands. They were blown up into the air, dancing wildly.

"Miss!" Yinxin cried again. She threw herself onto the grave and discovered that the soil was dry and warm. Suddenly, she understood that Yingtai had planned this ever since Shanbo's death. That was why she appeared to be so calm and confident after she had said good-bye to Shanbo. A mysterious power definitely helped to make all this happen.

The rain had stopped. Yinxin rose slowly. Somehow, she was not sad or afraid any more. She looked up, and saw the pink and blue cloth fragments still dancing in the air. She noticed that they seemed to be getting more colorful as they continued to dance. She looked more closely and saw that they had transformed into butterflies. One was pink, and the other blue.

Yinxin held her head up, fixing her eyes upon the butterflies, fascinated by their charm and grace. They turned and flew down toward her. Yinxin reached out to catch them, but they flew from under her arm and spiraled around. They flew close to her, but would not let her touch them. Finally, they flew further away and disappeared into the trees.

Yinxin stood there in amazement. Gradually, a sense of tranquility came over her. The whole thing felt like a dream, but she knew it had been real for Yingtai.

She ran all the way back to tell Gongyuan Zhu and Mrs. Zhu.

"Yinxin, where's Yingtai? It was such heavy rain!" Yinxin looked up to find the Zhus standing in front of her.

"She jumped into the grave." Yinxin did not know how else to tell them so she decided to be direct.

"Are you out of your mind?" said Gongyuan Zhu angrily, "Why would she do that? How could she possibly do that?"

"She spoke the truth. Miss Zhu did run into the grave." The five servants from the Ma family had now come back from the cemetery. One of them gave the Zhus a more detailed account.

"We followed Miss Zhu to the grave, but kept away from her at a distance. It began to rain so heavily that we were worried about her. We decided to go up to her and make sure that she was all right. We arrived just in time to see her jump into the grave. Yinxin tried to grasp her, but only managed to tear off two small pieces from her clothes. When Yinxin let go of them, they turned into butterflies and flew into the forest."

Mrs. Zhu was not prepared to accept such a story. "You all sound insane. You had better go and dry yourselves. I will stay and look for Yingtai."

Mrs. Zhu and Gongyuan Zhu walked to Shanbo's grave. "Oh, my, two gravestones!" Mrs. Zhu blurted out. "One for Shanbo, the other for Yingtai!"

"Who could have made the one for Yingtai. She just got here!" Gongyuan Zhu exclaimed.

"I was wondering where Yingtai was when it was raining so heavily. I could never dream of her going inside the grave! Isn't this all a nightmare?" Mrs. Zhu started to cry.

"Yingtai, Yingtai, come back!" She tried to dig into the grave, but the soil was hard and not removable.

Gongyuan Zhu was also in tears. He did not say a word, but kept digging into the grave with his hands like a mad man. Soon, his hands were red with blood, but the soil did not give in.

"What on earth has happened? Where is my daughter?" Mrs. Zhu screamed in a heartbreaking voice. She hit the grave hard with her fists and head. Then she passed out.

Gongyuan Zhu cried out, "Is this punishment for me? I did all this in the best interest of my daughter!" He knelt down in front of the grave and hit himself violently.

Yinxin and some of the servants from the Ma family arrived just in time to stop Gongyuan Zhu's self-abuse. They then rushed to Mrs. Zhu who was covered in tears and mud.

"Look, here come the butterflies again!" Someone shouted, pointing to the grave.

The pink butterfly with colorful spots was emerging from one side of the gravestone near its top. As it reached the top, a larger butterfly, a blue one with colorful spots on its wings, also appeared. They met at the top of the grave, touching each other several times and then flew over the grave. A ray of sunlight shone upon them.

Everyone held their breath as they watched their movements. "How beautiful!" "This is amazing!" A few people cried in admiration.

The butterflies seemed to understand. They came down to rest on the grave, and fluttered their wings for all to see. They flew up over the heads of Gongyuan Zhu and Mrs. Zhu, stopping briefly to flutter against their faces before they disappeared into the forest. With the butterflies gone, everyone stood there motionless, not knowing what to do.

Gongyuan Zhu was in a wretched state. "I guess there is nothing we can do now except going home. Those of you from the Ma family have seen what has happened and shall report to your masters."

After the Ma people had left, Mrs. Zhu insisted on staying to find out more about Yingtai. Since she could not be persuaded to go anywhere, Gongyuan Zhu and Yinxin had to stay with her for another day in the forest. She became extremely exhausted and fell sick at the end of that day, so Gongyuan Zhu decided to make their way home. Lying in bed half conscious, Mrs. Zhu kept blaming herself for separating Yingtai and Shanbo. Yinxin managed to convince her that Yingtai would go home herself if she were still alive. Gongyuan Zhu remained silent during the whole return trip, too confused and despairing to say anything.

EPILOGUE

THE ZHU FAMILY was never the same. Mrs. Zhu remained bedridden ever since the event at Shanbo's grave. Gongyuan Zhu refused to leave his room. Both of them seemed to have fallen under a spell.

With Yingtai gone, Yinxin literally had nothing to do in the family. A month later, she said good-bye to the old couple and left the Zhu house for good.

One day during the first spring after Shanbo and Yingtai were gone, Yinxin and Sijiu showed up in Huqiao county. They went straight to Nine Dragon Cemetery, to the small forest where their Miss and Master lay. They had with them a single large headstone with the inscription engraved upon it:

Shanbo Liang and Yingtai Zhu, Together at Last

They knelt down in their heavy mourning clothes and prayed. They then began to install the new gravestone in front of the grave.

As they were digging, they both felt something touching them on the face. Looking up, they saw two butterflies, the same ones Yinxin saw on the last day she was with Miss Zhu.

Yinxin and Sijiu stood in awe watching. The butterflies flew to the top of the grave where little flowers were in full bloom. Of all varied flowers that grew there, the pink ones and blue ones were the most attractive and fragrant.

"They are the incarnations of Miss Zhu and Master Liang," said Yingtai.

"I know. Look how happy and free they are! No one can stop them from going anywhere," Sijiu said enviously.

"That is what they had always desired," Yinxin said. Tears came into her eyes as she remembered all the experiences she had shared with Yingtai.

"We should feel happy for them," said Sijiu, holding Yinxin's hands tightly in his.

"Miss Zhu and Master Liang, Sijiu and I are together now. We will take care of both of your parents till their end."

"Please give us your blessing," Sijiu said.

They both knelt and looked up. The butterflies came down to give them each a touch on the head, and then they danced merrily in front of their eyes for a while. They were exceptionally graceful and beautiful.

Yinxin and Sijiu held out their hands for the butterflies to land on. The pink one came to Yinxin and the blue one to Sijiu. Yinxin and Sijiu were thrilled and played gently with their wings.

After a while, the blue butterfly flapped its wings and left Sijiu's palm. In response to that, the pink butterfly bade Yinxin good-bye by fluttering its wings. It flew upwards to join its partner. They rubbed each other intimately and glided side by side around the grave, around Yinxin and Sijiu.

Under the blue sky, above the flowers, around the bushes and trees, the two butterflies danced blissfully together. They flew high and low, farther and near. Eventually they fluttered away from the grave, took to the air, and faded into two kaleidoscopic dots in the cosmic distance.

As far as the human eye could see, the pink and blue specks melted into each other, creating an expanding fusion of heavenly beauty...

More titles from Homa & Sekey Books

Flower Terror: Suffocating Stories of China by Pu Ning
(ISBN 0-9665421-0-X, Fiction, Paperback, $13.95)

Acclaimed Chinese writer eloquently describes the oppression of intellectuals in his country between 1950s and 1970s in these twelve autobiographical novellas and short stories. Many of the stories are so shocking and heart-wrenching that one cannot but feel suffocated.

In "A Glass of Water," neighbors ignore a feverish old woman's pleas for water because her son has been denounced as counter-revolutionary. In "The Fossil," a wife does not speak to her writer husband for three years, because he is under suspicion. The title story portrays the absurdity of the period in which flowers seemed so alien to the oppressive political atmosphere that they evoked a sense of terror in people's mind and heart.

The Peony Pavilion: A Novel by Xiaoping Yen
(ISBN 0-9665421-2-6, Fiction, Paperback, $16.95)

A sixteen-year-old girl visits a forbidden garden and falls in love with a young man she meets in a dream. She has an affair with her dream-lover and dies longing for him. After her death, her unflagging spirit continues to wait for her dream-lover. Does her lover really exist? Can a youthful love born of a garden dream ever blossom?

Based on a famous sixteenth-century Chinese opera written by Tang Xianzu, "the Shakespeare of China," the novel leads the reader into a mythical world of passion and romance. Its many fascinating characters include a failed scholar, a Taoist nun, a husband and wife rebel team, a dissolute emperor, and Tartar invaders from the North.

More titles from Homa & Sekey Books

Always Bright: Paintings by American Chinese Artists 1970-1999 edited by Xue Jian Xin, Zhou Yong, Li Ning, Shawn Ye (ISBN 0-9665421-3-4, Art, Hardcover, $49.95)

A selection of paintings by eighty acclaimed American Chinese artists in the late twentieth century, *Always Bright* is the first of its kind in English publication. The album falls into three categories: oil painting, Chinese painting and other media painting. It also offers profiles of the artists and information on their professional accomplishment. The book fills a blank in the American Chinese art book publication and satisfies an increasing need from readers who crane to know American Chinese artists and their art.

Artists whose works are included in the album come from different back-grounds, use different media and belong to different schools. Some of them are veterans of the fascinating world of artistic creation who enjoy national and international fame, such as the famous Ling Nan School artist Ting Shao Kuang and oil painter Chen Yifei, while others are enterprising young men and women who are more impressionable to novelty and singularity.

www.homabooks.com

Order Information: Please send a check or money order (payable to Homa & Sekey Books) for each ordered book plus $3.50 shipping & handling to: Orders Department, Homa & Sekey Books, 138 Veterans Plaza, P.O. Box 103, Dumont, NJ 07628.